THE BEVERLY GRAY
MYSTERY STORIES

D1127871

BEVERLY GRAY'S QUEST

The BEVERLY GRAY *Mystery Stories*

By CLAIR BLANK

BEVERLY GRAY, FRESHMAN
BEVERLY GRAY, SOPHOMORE
BEVERLY GRAY, JUNIOR
BEVERLY GRAY, SENIOR
BEVERLY GRAY'S CAREER
BEVERLY GRAY ON A WORLD CRUISE
BEVERLY GRAY IN THE ORIENT
BEVERLY GRAY ON A TREASURE HUNT
BEVERLY GRAY'S RETURN
BEVERLY GRAY, REPORTER
BEVERLY GRAY'S ROMANCE
BEVERLY GRAY'S QUEST
BEVERLY GRAY'S PROBLEM
BEVERLY GRAY'S ADVENTURE
BEVERLY GRAY'S CHALLENGE
BEVERLY GRAY'S JOURNEY
BEVERLY GRAY'S ASSIGNMENT
BEVERLY GRAY'S MYSTERY
BEVERLY GRAY'S VACATION
BEVERLY GRAY'S FORTUNE
BEVERLY GRAY'S SECRET
BEVERLY GRAY'S ISLAND MYSTERY
BEVERLY GRAY'S DISCOVERY

"THERE IS A MEDICAL MISSIONARY THERE WHO WOULD HELP US."

Beverly Gray's Quest *Frontispiece* (*Page 124*)

The Beverly Gray College Mystery Series

BEVERLY GRAY'S QUEST

By CLAIR BLANK

GROSSET & DUNLAP

Publishers NEW YORK

Printed in the United States of America

Contents

CHAPTER		PAGE
I	An Offer	9
II	Plans	17
III	Detour	24
IV	Spirits	34
V	Lenora and the Bear	42
VI	San Francisco	59
VII	Lost	68
VIII	Beginning the Search	78
IX	The Fallen *Red Bird*	91
X	A Discovery	106
XI	Captives	116
XII	Beverly's Plan	126
XIII	Alone	131
XIV	Rescue	140
XV	Homeward Bound	153
XVI	The *Susabella*	167
XVII	A Mission	181
XVIII	The Brown Envelope	194
XIX	Home Again	211

BEVERLY GRAY'S QUEST

CHAPTER I

An Offer

It was a bright sunny morning, one of the last days of summer. The boy on the bicycle pedaled leisurely, his shrill but happy whistle bringing smiles from passers-by. Before a brownstone house he stopped and rested his bicycle against the curb. He removed his hat and from it drew a pencil, a small black book, and the telegram he had come to deliver.

As he approached the house the front door opened and a tanned, slim, slightly smiling girl appeared.

"Does Beverly Gray live here?" the boy asked, consulting the name on the telegram in his hand.

The girl paused in the act of drawing on her gloves. "I'm Beverly Gray."

"Telegram. Sign there."

The boy thrust his book at her and when she had signed it he went away whistling. Beverly looked dubiously at the yellow envelope in her hand. What could it be? She tore the envelope and extracted the single sheet of paper. She read the printed words, a faint frown wrinkling her forehead. Then she whirled and ran into the house, taking the stairs two at a time. She burst in upon her friends waving the telegram.

"Guess what!" she commanded.

The three girls seated at the breakfast table looked up with various expressions of surprise.

"It is too early in the morning for guessing games," Lenora Whitehill declared.

"Somebody has left you a million dollars," Lois Mason ventured.

"Good news, Bev?" Shirley Parker asked.

"Good news!" Beverly echoed. "It is glorious—marvelous—the best thing that ever happened——"

"It must be a million dollars," Lois laughed. "What else could make you happy so early in the morning?"

"Don't keep us in suspense," Lenora yawned. "Tell us quickly."

"It is my book——" Beverly said. "My publishers had told me weeks ago that there was a prospect of selling it to the movies. This telegram confirms it and they suggest that I go to Hollywood and collaborate on the scenario."

"You mean the movies—in Hollywood?" Lenora demanded. "California?"

Beverly looked at the telegram and nodded. "Mr. Stone has sold them the idea and all arrangements have been made. They suggest I go out and help in adapting the book for the screen."

"Are you?" Lois asked.

"Of course she is," Lenora returned. "This is just what she has been waiting for. Fame is practically on her doorstep."

"It is wonderful, Bev," Shirley added.

"I'm not famous yet, however," Beverly laughed with a glance at her watch, "and Mr. Blaine is not a patient man. *Tribune,* here I come!"

"Tell your editor I'll have those pictures of the fire for him this morning," Lenora called after her friend.

Hurrying downtown, Beverly thought about the telegram in her handbag. There was an urge within her to go to Hollywood and have even the smallest part in launching her book into this new field.

What would Larry say? She looked at the diamond ring sparkling on her left hand. After a week it was still new and a bit unbelievable. Larry—White Corners—and her happiness—all securely tied together.

All morning Beverly went about lighthearted and gay. When she met Larry for lunch she could scarcely suppress the news until they were seated in a restaurant and had given their orders to the waiter. Then she silently handed him the telegram and waited while he read it. He looked up and smiled.

"It's great, Beverly. Just what you wanted. I'm happy for you."

"It is a little unbelievable," Beverly confessed with a laugh. "To think of my book being one of those chosen—out of the thousands that are published every year!"

"It is an excellent book," Larry said. He tapped the telegram. "This proves it. You deserve every bit of it. Are you going out to California?"

"I don't know," Beverly said. "I haven't decided yet. It was just thrilling to think about——"

"It is what you have worked for," he said.

"But I've something else now," Beverly said. "There's White Corners——"

"And me," Larry finished, smiling. "We'll always wait for you, Bev. If you want to go to Hollywood and——"

"Holding hands in broad daylight!" A strange, laughing voice declared.

"Mike!" Larry cried, leaping up and shaking the newcomer's hand enthusiastically. "Sit down with us. Beverly, this is Michael McKay. He was my roommate in college."

A pair of twinkling black eyes laughed down at Beverly from a tanned, rugged face under a shock of unruly hair. His smile was delightful and lighted his whole countenance.

"Larry has told me so much about you, Mr. McKay," Beverly said as Mike slid onto the extra chair the waiter produced.

"I've been hearing about you, too," was the frank rejoinder, "so I came to see who Larry had gotten himself engaged to. Now that I've seen you he has my approval. All the happiness in the world to both of you. Sure, from the looks of your smilin' faces you've got a good slice of it already."

"When Mike gets excited his Irish ancestors pop up in him, hence the brogue," Larry informed her. "Mike, what are you doing in New York? The last time I heard of you you were a test pilot down in Texas."

"I was that for almost two years," Mike returned. "Then I got a berth on a freighter and sailed around South America. A very interesting country, that. While I was there I heard the story. That's why I came looking for you."

"What story?" Larry asked. "What does it have to do with me?"

"It is your chance for adventure," Mike said, hitching his chair a little closer. "It is a beauty spot the like of which you've never seen. Orchids growing wild——"

"Get to the point, Mike."

"The point is the emerald."

"Emerald!" Beverly echoed.

"So big it takes two men to lift it," he assured her solemnly.

"Oh, come, Mike," Larry laughed. "Where did you ever hear that story?"

"From one of the natives," Mike said. "I did something for him once—saved his life as a matter of fact. I know he wasn't misleading me. He told me about it and approximately where it is."

"If he knows, why doesn't he get it?" Larry interposed.

"The natives are superstitious about the section of land where the emerald lies—witchcraft or some such nonsense. Look, Larry, I've sketched a map. With a plane we could land easily on the flat portion of plateau and——"

"We?" Larry interrupted.

"You and I," Mike said.

"Wait a minute!" Larry laughed. "In about three weeks I start on a new job behind a shiny desk and with my own secretary. I can't go galloping around South America. Besides, what gave you this idea?"

"Two of my best friends went to find the emerald. They never came back. I want to know what happened to them. I thought since you have your own plane——" Mike looked hopefully from Larry to Beverly. "We could probably do it in three weeks," he offered.

As Mike talked Beverly could see that Larry was beginning to waver. He listened, occasionally asking a question which Mike eagerly explained. It seemed Mike had considered every possibility. At last Larry looked across at Beverly, eyes twinkling.

"What do you think, Beverly?"

"Mike makes it very interesting," Beverly smiled. "I'd almost like to go myself."

"It is only for three weeks," added Larry, "and if you go to California——"

"Then you agree?" Mike asked eagerly. "I'll make all the arrangements."

"If we go we will use the *Red Bird III,*" Larry said, "but I haven't committed myself yet. I want to think it over."

CHAPTER II

Plans

"How long does it take to drive to California?" Shirley asked musingly, putting down her newspaper.

"Oh—about a week, I guess," Lenora returned. Then, hopefully: "Why?"

"I was just wondering," Shirley said, retreating behind her paper.

"Are you by any chance reading the travel advertisements?" Lenora inquired. "All about the sunny beaches and starlit nights, the tall, whispering redwoods and old mission bells in the moonlight——"

"The sparkling blue Pacific," mused Shirley.

"Stop! You're breaking my heart!" Lois cried. "I couldn't possibly get off to go with you——"

"Who's going?" Shirley demanded. "I merely asked——"

"But Lenora spent all morning picking out clothes and she said——" Lois began.

"Quiet!" Lenora shouted. At Shirley's glance she murmured, "I only thought we might go with Beverly."

"Beverly isn't sure that she is going," Shirley pointed out.

"Here she comes. We'll ask her," Lois declared. She left the kitchen where she had been setting the table for their evening meal and went into the living room to greet her friend as the front door slammed.

"Beverly, come out and settle the question. Are you or are you not going to California?"

"At this point it looks as though I am," Beverly laughed. "Why?"

"By some strange coincidence Shirley and I are going too," Lenora said.

"You are?"

"We feel that a jaunt across the country is just what we

need," Lenora continued. "Shirley has been trying to persuade me to go in her car——"

"I didn't say a word," Shirley protested with a laugh, "but it is a good idea."

"And I was afraid I would have to go alone," Beverly sighed. "It's wonderful."

"We can see the Grand Canyon and Yellowstone Park and Boulder Dam and——"

"They are not in California—in case you are interested," Lois pointed out.

"They are on the way," Lenora returned. "Gosh, I can hardly believe we are really going. What will Larry do while you are gone, Bev?"

"He is flying to South America with a friend of his on an exploring expedition."

"Exploring? You mean like Columbus?" Lenora wanted to know. "What do they expect to find?"

"A fortune," Beverly laughed. "But they won't be too disappointed if they don't find it. They want adventure more than anything else."

"Hm. Maybe I would rather go with them," Lenora said thoughtfully. "Who is Larry's friend?"

"His name is Michael McKay," Beverly replied. "He was Larry's roommate in college."

"South America is beginning to call more loudly," Lenora murmured. "Has he by any chance dark eyes and curly hair?"

"He has," Beverly laughed.

"Lenora!" Shirley exclaimed. "You have been talking California for days. If you back out now——"

"I won't," Lenora laughed. "I was just asking."

"We know you," put in Lois. "I can see that Terry should never have gone to England."

"Let's have dinner," Lenora said abruptly. The subject of Terry and his departure to fight for his country was one she refused to discuss, and the other girls believed it to be because his going had meant more to her than she cared to have anyone know.

"If we really intend to drive out to the coast we'll have to start making plans," Shirley said. "We'll have to leave soon because in a month or so *Lonesome Lady* is reopening and I'll have to be back for rehearsals."

"Don't you think it is dangerous?" Lois asked.

"Why?" Lenora shot at her.

"Well, three girls alone—driving all that way——"

"Tush! Haven't you heard? There aren't any more wild Indians," Lenora said.

"I'm almost afraid to ask Charlie Blaine for a leave of absence," Beverly mused.

"He will probably have a fit," Lenora giggled.

"Unless you could convince him it is a great chance for some feature articles for his paper," Lois said.

"My chum, that is a priceless idea!" Lenora exclaimed. "Why didn't I think of it? Beverly could write stories about the things we see and I could take pictures."

"A sort of diary," added Shirley.

"It might work," Beverly agreed slowly.

"Let's go down and talk to him," Lenora proposed.

"Tonight?"

"Certainly. What say, Bev?" Lenora replied brightly.

"All right," Beverly agreed, "but I think we'll have a hard time convincing him."

Lenora and Beverly departed for the *Tribune* office immediately after dinner. Charlie Blaine was looking over proof sheets and another man was hovering in the background when the girls entered the office.

"May we talk to you for a few minutes, Mr. Blaine?" Beverly asked.

"We have a great idea," added Lenora.

"Whatever it is—no!" Blaine said, frowning. He handed the proof sheets to the man waiting and turned back to his desk. "I'm busy."

"This is important," Lenora insisted. "It is about our cross-country diary."

"Your what? Is this another one of your ideas like counting the hairs in a rabbit's tail or digging for sunken treasure in the Hudson River?"

Lenora and Beverly laughed together. It was true that Lenora had approached the editor before with enthusiastic plans which, after more careful consideration, had proved impractical. It was small wonder then that he viewed this latest development with suspicion.

"We are going to California," Lenora explained, "and we thought——"

"California!" Blaine echoed. He turned to the other girl. "Beverly, what is all this?"

Beverly showed him the telegram she had received and explained the situation. Because he had always been interested in her writing career, even before her graduation from Vernon College, he heartily commended her now.

"It is an opportunity that might lead to a great number of things," he said at last. "I think you should go."

"Mr. Blaine," Lenora said, eyes dancing with mischief, "I could kiss you. We knew you would understand."

"He has always understood," Beverly said gratefully. "He gave me a chance when I had no experience and taught me everything I know."

"Bosh!" said Blaine crisply, but the girls knew that he was pleased. "No one can bring out something that isn't there. You've a talent for writing, Beverly. It will drive you and possess you—might even make you unhappy sometimes, but don't let anything stop you. Then, some day, I can say I knew you when." He turned back to his desk. "Now go away. I'm busy."

As they were going out the door he called:

"Those stories and pictures had better be good or don't bother to come to the office when you get back."

"He is as bristly as a porcupine on the outside but he has a heart of gold," Lenora declared as they left the *Tribune* building. "Just think, Bev, we are on our way to California!"

CHAPTER III

Detour

WHITE CORNERS stood surrounded with the vivid colors of late summer. The trees in the drive were beginning to turn scarlet and yellow and at one side of the house, beside the French windows leading into the library, chrysanthemums hung heavy heads in the sunlight.

"It is the most beautiful spot ever," Beverly whispered. "I already feel as if it has belonged to us always."

Larry smiled down at her. "Happy?"

"So happy I'm a little afraid," Beverly said, her voice trembling. "Larry, we have so much, doesn't it make you hold your breath sometimes? If it could only last forever!"

"It will last forever," he said, holding out his hand. "Nothing shall ever part us, Beverly. Nothing, I promise you."

"Hey, Larry! You've got a family of squirrels in the oak tree." Roger and Shirley dashed around the corner of the house, hand in hand, laughing.

"It is a lovely place, Beverly," Shirley declared. "No wonder you are both so proud of it."

"We've been looking at the house across the road," added Roger. "It is empty."

"You mean you might buy it?" Beverly asked gleefully. "We'd be neighbors!"

"We don't know if it is for sale," Shirley murmured. "Anyway—we'll see."

They climbed into Roger's car and as it started out the driveway, Beverly cried:

"Roger, wait!" She turned around to take another last look at the white house shining in the setting sun.

"What's wrong?" Larry asked.

"I don't know," Beverly said, suppressing a shiver.

"Just suddenly I felt afraid—it was like a shadow—a premonition that we might never see it again."

"Silly!" Larry murmured gently. "Tomorrow you leave for California and Mike and I for South America. White Corners will be here waiting—for both of us."

Beverly was only partly reassured by his words. There still persisted that feeling of impending disaster, though she said no more about it to the others throughout their gay evening.

Larry and Mike were to take off at dawn and the girls planned to start about seven o'clock. Therefore, they retired early but there was little sleep for anyone. Lenora was so excited she kept Shirley and Lois awake, and Beverly was wakeful on her own account because of that gloomy foreboding.

At last in desperation Beverly got up and dressed.

"Where are you going at this hour?" Shirley asked sleepily.

"To the airport. May I borrow your car?"

"Help yourself," Shirley yawned. "Call me when you get back."

When Beverly turned the car onto the Queensboro Bridge the first faint pink glow of daylight was just beginning to tip the horizon. Streets were deserted and the air was clear and cold. As she came onto the landing field a man left the side of a small red plane and came toward her. Beverly stepped out of the car and stood waiting.

"Beverly!" Larry exclaimed. "I didn't expect you. We said good-bye last night——"

"This is a postscript," Beverly laughed. "I—I just wanted to see you take off."

"That funny feeling again?" he asked.

She nodded. "I can't help it, Larry. Be careful."

"Same to you," he directed smilingly. "Stay away from those handsome movie actors. I'll see you in a month or so and write you in care of General Delivery in Los Angeles."

Out on the field the motor of the plane broke into a roar, and Mike waved a gay hand.

"Good-bye, darling." For a second Larry held her hand tightly, then kissed her and strode off to climb aboard the *Red Bird III*.

Beverly watched until the little plane was lost in the low-hanging clouds, then she climbed back into Shirley's car and returned to the apartment, determined to shake off that foreboding.

She found the girls up and dressed, though not very wide awake.

"It is a good thing you don't go away every day," Lois yawned. "I'd be a nervous wreck."

"You can sleep every morning from now on until we get back," Lenora said blithely. "You won't see us for a month or more."

"I'll miss you," Lois said, unexpectedly serious.

"We'll miss you too," Beverly returned.

"I wish you were going with us," added Shirley.

"I'll keep the home fires burning," Lois replied. "Heavens! That reminds me—the toast!"

The girls from upstairs, Hope Rodgers, Connie Elwood, Kathleen Ryan and Virginia Harris wandered down in pajamas and housecoats to see the travelers off. Baggage was stored in place and Lenora climbed in the back seat with her camera and supply of maps and sightseeing folders. Shirley was at the wheel with Beverly beside her.

"California or bust!" Lenora shouted as the car began to move. "Good-bye, everybody!"

"We are actually on our way," Shirley said, settling herself more comfortably. "I can hardly believe it."

"Bound for the wide open spaces," sighed Beverly.

"With three thousand miles ahead of us," added Lenora happily. "What a trip this will be!"

The sun shone with pleasant intentness and the ride to Renville, Beverly's home town and their first overnight stop, was enjoyable but uneventful. They pulled up before the Gray home early in the afternoon and all their friends were on hand to welcome them. There were Beverly's parents, Anne, who had been in college with them, and her husband and young son. In addition there were the other members of the Lucky Circle, a group of young people of the town with whom Beverly had been very popular and whom Shirley and Lenora had met on previous visits to Renville.

The Lucky Circle had planned a big evening for them. They had provided a huge wagon filled with straw and drawn by a team of sturdy horses to take the whole group beyond the town for a barbecue.

When the food had disappeared the young people sat around the campfire and sang songs and told stories. Lenora, at her best as a story teller, held them enchanted with a ghostly tale until it seemed the very woods around them contained mysterious eyes and figures and the rustling leaves were specters whispering to one another.

"I know it is silly," Barbara West said with a nervous glance over her shoulder, "but I feel as if someone were watching us."

"It's the ghosts," Joan Roberts giggled. "Lenora has roused them with her story."

"I'm surprised at you," Lenora laughed. "Don't you know there aren't any such things as ghosts?"

"Don't you believe in ghosts?" Boyd Marshall asked interestedly.

"Of course not," Lenora said.

"So she doesn't believe in ghosts!" Gordon Brewster pulled Boyd aside as the talk became general and all the way back to Renville the two plotted in secret.

The next morning the girls resumed their journey full of gaiety and good spirit. After they had gone about fifty miles dark clouds gathered overhead and rain pelted on the roof. Lenora played records on the portable phonograph she had insisted on bringing with her and beamed on her friends.

"Isn't this cozy?"

Beverly and Shirley, straining their eyes to see the rain-swept highway, permitted themselves a brief smile. It was no easy task to guide the car over an unfamiliar road in a storm. It made the situation even worse when they came to a detour.

"A detour!" Lenora groaned. "Now we are sure to be lost."

"The map doesn't show a detour," Beverly added, frowning intently over the maze of blue lines.

"Ouch! What a bump!" Lenora cried as the car lurched heavily.

"Look at that road! A sea of mud. It must have been raining here for days. All we need now is—oh!" Shirley gasped.

"What's wrong?" Lenora leaned over the seat.

"Look at the gauge. We are almost out of gas."

"But I thought we filled it last night in Renville," Beverly said.

"We did," Shirley nodded.

"That's strange," Lenora declared. "There must be termites in the gas tank."

"Whatever it is certainly eats gasoline," Shirley sighed. "Uh-oh, there it goes."

The engine coughed and died into silence. The starter whirled merrily but the engine did not start.

"Lost on a detour in a cloudburst," Lenora sighed. "I

can think of nicer things. Here is a story for your first day, Bev."

"But how am I going to send it from here and what shall it be about?" Beverly demanded.

"The rain drenched countryside held unsuspected beauty——" Lenora began when Shirley interrupted.

"There is a house over there."

"Where?"

The other two girls turned to stare out the window.

"Goody! Maybe it is haunted!" Lenora said gleefully. "Let's go see if we can get some gasoline."

"What would ghosts be doing with gasoline?" Shirley wanted to know disgustedly.

"Well—maybe the witches ride gasoline scooters instead of broomsticks. After all, these modern inventions——"

"Let's go and see if anyone lives there," Beverly suggested.

"In all this rain?" Shirley demurred. "Oh, very well, if I must."

"It is a good thing we didn't pack our raincoats," Lenora declared, passing Beverly her coat and then Shirley hers.

"We'll need our galoshes to cross that field," Shirley

declared. "Couldn't we just sit here until someone comes along the road?"

"We have been here twenty minutes now and there hasn't been one single car," Beverly pointed out.

"Come on," Lenora urged. "You won't melt."

CHAPTER IV

Spirits

THEY stepped out onto the road. The mud oozed under their feet and rain blew at them in great gusts.

"I'll wait in the car," Shirley said, climbing back inside.

"Oh, no, you don't!" Lenora laughed. "You own the car that ran out of gas, so you'll come along!"

"Okay," Shirley sighed and climbed out again reluctantly.

They left the road and started across a field. The wind whipped about them and swept them breathless.

"Hang the old car anyway!" Shirley grumbled. "Of all places to run out of gas. I don't understand it."

"We may not be daisies but we are certainly getting well watered," Lenora added, brushing a drop of water from the tip of her nose.

"The house looks deserted," Beverly murmured as they approached the gray frame building.

"It will be a shelter from the storm anyway," Shirley said.

They mounted the broken, worn steps to the porch. Boards were rotted away and the girls moved slowly and cautiously.

"Let's go inside," Lenora proposed. "Anything will be better than standing in the rain."

They approached the front door and it swung open untouched. The girls exchanged surprised glances and Shirley played the light from her flashlight over the threshold. Hesitantly they stepped inside. The door closed behind them and the damp darkness of the deserted house pressed close on all sides.

"I don't like this," Lenora said with a shiver.

"Like this!" It was an eerie echo.

"I think I prefer the rain," Shirley said and hastily retraced her steps to the door.

"We are at least dry in here," Beverly said. "We can

wait until the rain stops and then go on to the next house."

"Well—" Shirley conceded doubtfully as the wind howled about the house.

From somewhere came a loud banging noise.

"Complete with banging shutters," Lenora said with a nervous chuckle. "What a house to haunt."

"Let's see how many other rooms there are," Beverly proposed.

"You think of the nicest things!" Lenora grumbled, but nevertheless she closely followed her friends.

The three rooms on the ground floor were heavy with dust and deserted. They were about to go upstairs when Lenora called a halt.

"Sh-h-h!"

"What's the matter?" Shirley asked in a startled whisper.

"I heard something."

"Only the wind," Beverly said calmly.

"Perhaps. I guess—no, there it is again!" Lenora cried. "Oh, me! We've done it again."

"Done what?" Shirley wanted to know.

"Walked into another haunted house," Lenora replied.

"You are the girl who said there weren't such things as ghosts," Beverly reminded. "Have you changed your mind?"

"N-no," Lenora said at last. "But still—there it goes again."

"I don't hear a thing but the wind," Shirley said with a frown. "You're dreaming."

"If I'm dreaming you are, too," Lenora declared. "You're with me."

"Wait!" Beverly held up her hand. "I heard it that time—a sound as if chains were being dragged across a floor."

"That settles it!" Shirley started toward the door. "Good-bye, girls, I'll see you in California."

"You've got to stay with us—you've got the flashlight." Lenora firmly gripped her friend's arm.

"Here—you can have it." Shirley thrust out the flashlight and Beverly took it while Lenora maintained a clasp on Shirley's arm.

There came to them the unmistakable sound of heavy footsteps.

"Uh-oh!"

"Sh-h-h!" Beverly warned.

She played the small circle of light from the flashlight

hastily around the room. They stood in the center of what probably once had been the dining room. They had just come from the kitchen and beyond lay the living room through which they had first entered. All of them were deserted.

"Ohhhh!" A wail rose from somewhere in the house and the three girls shivered.

"Beverleee! Shirleeee! Lenorrrra!"

"Whoever it is knows our names!" Lenora said in startled surprise.

"Of course I know your names." A deep, hollow voice echoed in the room. "I know everything," it declared.

"What in the world——" Shirley began.

"Who are you?" Lenora wanted to know.

"I am a great spirit," the voice continued. "Some call me a ghost."

The words died into eerie silence while the three girls stood frozen in their places.

"You three are here today for judgment. One of you—indeed all three of you—have scoffed at the idea of spirits, voicing loudly your disbelief in the things of my world. Now you will see. Prepare yourselves——"

The light in Beverly's hand danced hastily around the

room. Certainly there was no one visible here in the room with them, yet the voice came from here—right beside them! Then, overhead, in the ceiling, she caught a glimpse of a small square iron grating. In old houses, she knew, these iron grill registers had been used in heating the houses. They permitted the heat to rise to the second floor from the first. There had been one like this in her grandmother's house.

"Keep him talking," Beverly whispered to Shirley and switched off the flashlight.

On tiptoe Beverly left the room and hesitated at the stairs leading to the floor above. If the steps creaked it would destroy her hope of surprising the "great spirit." Taking the stairs slowly and keeping close to the wall, one hand out to guide her, Beverly slowly mounted to the second floor.

When Beverly reached the top of the stairs she halted and strained her eyes to see through the gloomy darkness. She had an impulse to switch on the flashlight and see what lay about her, but she knew that at the first ray of light the ghost would be gone.

For a few minutes there was silence; then came the sound of muffled laughter, faint but unmistakable. Someone was having a hilarious time. Guided by her hearing and the touch of her hand on the wall, Beverly moved toward that laughter.

She came to the room directly over the dining room and paused in the doorway. Two figures were kneeling in the corner. As Beverly watched, one of them put a small microphone to his lips and assumed the deep, dramatic voice of the "great spirit."

"Thou art to——" he was beginning when the yellow circle of light from Beverly's flash fell upon them. He and his companion sprang up.

"Girls," Beverly called, "come upstairs and meet the 'great spirit.'"

There were hurried footsteps on the stairs and Shirley and Lenora burst into the room.

"Boyd!"

"Gordon!"

The two members of the Lucky Circle bowed laughingly.

"Don't shoot!" Boyd held up his hands in mock surrender.

"A trick! Of all the nerve—scaring us like that," Lenora began.

"Last night you said you didn't believe in ghosts," Gordon reminded. "We were simply testing you. This was such a good spot we couldn't resist it."

"How did you know we would stop here?" Beverly demanded.

"We—ah——" Boyd looked inquiringly at Gordon.

"You didn't by any chance drain some of the gasoline from our car?" Shirley continued.

"We followed you to make sure nothing happened to you," Gordon pointed out. "We're Chicago bound."

"But something is about to happen to you," Lenora declared. "In the next town you are going to take us to dinner. You scared an enormous appetite into me."

CHAPTER V

Lenora and the Bear

THE breezes from Lake Michigan swept the Boulevard with a cooling effect that was delicious after the long, hot drive. Lenora, leaning at a perilous angle from the window of the car, snapped the shutter of her camera triumphantly as they passed the Art Museum.

"Got it!"

In the roadster behind Shirley's car in the line of traffic Boyd tooted the horn gaily. The two cars had kept together since their occupants' meeting in the "haunted" house. At night they had stopped at the same hotels and had explored together any spots of interest they could find.

"Look at the boats on the lake!" Shirley exclaimed.

"Let's go for a boat ride," Lenora proposed. "I am so hot and dusty a ride on the lake would be just the thing!"

"I second the motion," Beverly agreed.

"Suppose we find our hotel first and get settled," Shirley proposed.

"It might be wise to have dinner, too," Lenora conceded.

"Food again!" Shirley shook her head. "What do you say, Beverly?"

"It's all right with me," Beverly nodded.

Chicago was familiar to the girls since they had been there before. Nevertheless they took a keen delight in sightseeing under Gordon's and Boyd's guidance, and Lenora took innumerable pictures which were sent with a story Beverly wrote to Charlie Blaine in the *Tribune* office in New York.

They tried to crowd everything possible into one day in Chicago. On the morning of the second day they bade farewell to their friends and headed the car westward.

It was a lovely day, warm as midsummer but with the colors of approaching autumn. No clouds marred the blanket of blue sky and the wind was only a gentle whisper.

"You know," Lenora remarked with a sigh, "I would make a wonderful hobo. The open road calls me. Ah, to do nothing but travel——"

"In box cars," interrupted Shirley, "with no full course dinners or stylish clothes——"

"You always look at the worst side," Lenora accused.

"I am only being practical," Shirley defended.

"Think how romantic the wandering, nomadic life would be. No work——"

"It is more romantic to have flowers and silverware on the table than to eat right out of the can," Shirley laughed. "Don't you agree, Beverly?"

"I certainly do," Beverly smiled. "Isn't it about time for lunch? While we eat we can study the map and decide where we will spend the night."

"I want to stay in a tourist cabin," Lenora decided. She flung her arms wide. "I crave the rugged life of wide open spaces."

"Rugged!" Shirley echoed, winking at Beverly. "We'll see what we can do."

They were entering a small town and decided to stop at a drugstore for luncheon. They spread their map out on the table to plan a stopover for the night. At this, the druggist and his assistant began to offer advice. A customer came into the store and he, too, came over to join the discussion. As a result, their lunch took them an hour longer than they had anticipated and they had to hurry to make their destination before nightfall.

"Ye Old Rustic Cabins" came into sight just as the sun dipped behind the horizon. Six little two-room log cabins, each with a bright red roof and white curtains at the windows, nestled cozily in a green valley.

"Aren't they cute?" Lenora exclaimed. "Let's take the one on the end."

Shirley drove off the highway and stopped before the largest cabin, evidently the home of the proprietor. A gray-haired, wiry little man came out to the car and greeted them with a friendly nod. Arrangements were soon completed and the girls installed in Lenora's choice of the small cabins.

"There doesn't seem to be anyone else in any of the other cabins," Shirley reported, coming in with the last suitcase.

"Then we can really be alone," Lenora said. "Girls! Come look! A real stone fireplace. They even furnish the wood and matches!"

There were two rooms, each with a large double bed. Lenora decided on a room all to herself and Beverly and Shirley shared the other.

Darkness came very rapidly, it seemed to the girls, and rather than sit in the glare of the bare electric bulb suspended from the ceiling, they yielded to Lenora's desire and built a fire in the fireplace. In the warm, flickering glow of this they sat and planned the next day's journey. At last, when the fire had died to smouldering embers, they went to bed and silence settled within the cabin.

In about a half-hour Beverly heard a "Pssst!" from the next room. She smiled but did not answer. After a moment it came again.

"Are you asleep?" Lenora asked in a loud whisper.

"How can we sleep?" Shirley retorted. "What do you want?"

"Do you hear that noise?" Lenora asked.

"Crickets," Beverly supplied.

"Do they do that all night?" Lenora demanded.

"Yes," Shirley said with a giggle, "they do that all night."

"How are we going to get any sleep?" Lenora demanded. "Isn't there any way to stop them?"

"Go to sleep and forget about them," Shirley advised. "Good night."

There was silence while Lenora thought over the problem of the crickets. Then:

"Beverly! Shirley! Did you hear that?"

"What is it this time?" Shirley asked with a sigh.

"Someone is trying to get in," Lenora hissed. "Hear him?"

"Imagination!" Shirley said, retreating again under the covers.

"I don't hear anything," added Beverly.

"There is someone at the door," Lenora insisted. "M—maybe it is an animal. A wolf, maybe. Or a bear."

"It is probably just a little termite making himself at home in the ceiling," Shirley mumbled sleepily.

"Suppose it is a bear and he chews the tires off your car," Lenora continued.

"A bear!" Shirley scoffed. "You're dreaming."

"But there is something out there," Lenora insisted.

"I'll go and see," Beverly offered, "or we'll never get any sleep."

"If you need help just scream," Lenora said.

Beverly opened the door and stood there silently for a

moment. The air was cool and fragrant. She could see hundreds of stars overhead and the white, deserted ribbon of highway beyond the section of green lawn. There was no sound of any kind. She left the door open and walked out to the car. There was no sign of life. She went back to report that all was well.

She had been in bed about five minutes when there was a scramble in the next room and Lenora let out a scream. Beverly and Shirley leaped from bed while sounds of a struggle and Lenora's piercing screams continued. They ran into their friend's room and, stumbling in the darkness, Beverly found the overhead light.

In the sudden glare the girls blinked and Lenora let out another shriek. From her one hand dangled a gray squirrel, squirming in fright while she clutched his bushy tail.

Lenora let go and the squirrel darted into the dark region under the bed. Beverly opened the door and the small creature scampered out into the night. Behind him he left chaos. Shirley was convulsed with laughter; Lenora was grinning foolishly and carefully caressing one injured finger; Beverly laughingly got out the first-aid kit.

"He probably came in when I opened the door to look for Lenora's bear," Beverly offered.

"Perhaps he had a store of nuts in the chimney," added Shirley.

"I don't see why he had to pick on my bed and wave his tail in my face," Lenora said frowning. "What did I ever do to him that he had to scare me so?"

"Every time I think of you holding that poor squirrel by the tail——" Shirley collapsed in a gale of laughter.

"Poor squirrel, nothing!" Lenora retorted. "He bit me."

"And you wanted the wild, primitive life," Shirley giggled. "Wait until the girls at home hear about this!"

"It ought to be good for a Sunday feature article in the *Tribune,*" added Beverly, eyes twinkling.

"If either of you dare to breathe a word of this," Lenora threatened, "I'll—I'll—well, I'll think of something," she added darkly.

They were on their way early the next morning. Each day seemed to bring something new. They traveled highways shaded and green, and some flat and dusty in the white glare of the sun. They grew travel-stained and weary. Sometimes their eyes ached from watching the ribbon of road unfold endlessly before them. At other times they came upon cool green spots and lingered dreamily to watch ducks on a pond or cows grazing peacefully in a wide meadow. They were seeing their America —the homes, the factories, the throbbing cities and peaceful farms, the might and richness of their native land— and their hearts swelled with pride at being a part of it.

The girls wasted very little time in stopovers at any of the points they visited. They had not planned a direct route across the country, preferring to deviate and see the spots which interested them, yet linger not too long in any one place. It meant many more miles of driving, but it meant more interesting experiences and adventures, too.

Their first important goal was Yellowstone Park.

"I want to see the bears," Lenora had told them firmly.

"We want the bears to see you," Beverly returned mischievously.

"But for goodness' sake, don't try holding one of them by the tail as you did that squirrel," Shirley giggled.

"Miss Parker," Lenora said coldly, "I shall ignore you."

At last on a cool sunny morning they entered Cody, Wyoming. They lunched leisurely and got their first glimpse of actual western scenes. They visited Buffalo

Bill's home and took pictures of the statue erected to his memory. Then they started the drive over the thrilling Cody Road, past the Shoshone Dam, through the Shoshone National Forest and the Stone Cliffs, where Lenora's imagination was put to active use in picking out fanciful figures formed by the stone. They passed great snow-dotted mountains, wide, flower-filled rolling meadows, more and more impressed with the beauty of the country.

They drove up to the Canyon Hotel just as the sun was setting. After getting settled and having dinner in the huge dining room, the girls wrote post cards to their friends at home. Later they took a bus trip to the bear feeding grounds where they watched grizzly bears and black bears, some with clumsy little cubs at their side, amble out of the forest to partake of the bits of food placed by the rangers. When it grew dark the girls returned to the hotel to enjoy the music in the lounge. It was there that Lenora got her brilliant idea.

"Let's take the sunrise trip to Mount Washburn."

"Sunrise?" Shirley inquired skeptically.

"We leave here at four o'clock in the morning," Lenora

continued enthusiastically. "We'll see the sunrise from the top of the mountain and see some big-horned sheep——"

"Can you guarantee a sunrise?" Beverly wanted to know.

"Yes," added Shirley, "suppose it rains?"

"Don't be so pessimistic," Lenora chided. "Let's go. We can have two breakfasts if we do."

"All right, but wait until you have to get up at three in the morning!" Shirley warned.

That gave Lenora pause for a moment. However, she tossed her head in disdain.

"I guess I can do it if you can."

When it came time to crawl out of bed in the dark, early morning it was Lenora who did the grunting and groaning, despite her words. They had doughnuts and hot chocolate in the spotless kitchen, and afterward climbed into their bus and were whisked away in the grayness of the morning.

It was cold on the mountain top, but they went into the snug little ranger cabin for warmth and chatted pleasantly with the forest man. The sun, when it appeared over the edge of the world, was a glory of gold and red.

Lenora, her precious camera loaded with color film, was busy all the while.

The girls returned to the hotel for breakfast and donned slacks for a hike to the bottom of the canyon. It was a two-mile walk from the hotel to the lodge where began the trail which led to the bottom of the waterfall. The descent was easily accomplished and they stood in the spray of the falls towering above them and marveled at the swift flow of water and the rainbow formed in the mist by the sun's rays. The walls of the canyon rose around them, great rocky cliffs, a myriad of blending colors. They lingered there, loath to leave the rushing water and beauty of the spot.

They took the climb back to the rim of the canyon in easy stages, stopping often to rest and admire the view. By the time they reached the hotel again they were hot and tired and more than ready for luncheon.

Immediately after lunch they left for Old Faithful, driving over wide, smooth roads, now and then catching glimpses of deer and bear in the woods.

They stopped briefly at Norris Geyser Basin and then at the Fountain Paint Pots to marvel at the geysers and the boiling springs.

The rugged, dark wood of the Old Faithful Inn was a contrast to the light juniper wood of the Canyon Hotel and, the girls felt, more symbolic of the west they had hoped to find.

They wasted little time indoors, for they were anxious to see Old Faithful in action. They had to wait several minutes for the geyser to perform, but when it did, they felt again wonder at the works of nature. The spouting white water and steam against the vivid blue sky was a scene they would always remember. That night, with the bright arc light playing on the geyser, it seemed even more impressive—a giant white fountain in the blackness of night, dimming even the glow of the stars in the milky way overhead.

The next morning they rose early to go horseback riding. The small, alert cow ponies, gentle and surefooted, trotted lightly over the narrow trails. Through pine-scented woods, cool and shadowed, across trickling, narrow streams, they rode to the foot of Mystic Falls, a swift mountain stream tumbling down a rocky bed. The beauty of the surrounding country was breathtaking—the coolness and silence, the narrow mountain trails and flat plains, the colorful wild flowers and the occasional twitter of birds mingled with the thud, thud of their ponies' hoofs.

"Ypeee!" Lenora yelled suddenly, breaking the silence.

Her horse reared and plunged ahead, startled. When she had quieted him she trotted meekly back into the single file of riders.

"I was only practicing to be a cow girl," she grinned.

"You'd make a right smart one, Ma'am," their cowboy guide laughed.

"You sounded more like a wild Indian," Shirley added.

That evening they attended an illustrated lecture in the open air amphitheater in back of the ranger station and went to bed early in preparation for their long drive the next day.

It was a cool, clear morning when they left Old Faithful and headed westward. They came to a spot where workmen had been busy cutting down trees to clear a parking area for automobiles. Lenora insisted that Shirley stop the car so that she could obtain a pine cone from the fallen tree, arguing that it was not defacing the beauty of the park since the tree was already destroyed.

Shirley stopped the car and the three girls got out. Lenora, a candy bar in one hand, was busily seeking a choice pine cone when she heard a stir in the underbrush and looked up to see a big black bear advancing toward her. The bear stood squarely in Lenora's path, blocking her retreat to the car and her friends. His nose wiggled inquisitively and his paws dabbed at the air. He squatted on his haunches, his eyes on Lenora.

"Beverly! Shirley!" The blonde girl shrieked. "Look at the bear!" Tales the ranger had told them the previous night ran through Lenora's head. It was not a common occurrence for bears to attack people without some provocation but it had been known to happen.

"You look at him," Shirley giggled unfeelingly, a few yards away. "He has his eye on you."

"Do something," Lenora cried. "I don't like the gleam in his eye."

"He is looking at your candy," Beverly called.

"Do you suppose he is vicious?" Lenora wanted to know.

"Animals are always unpredictable," was Shirley's comforting rejoinder. "He might take it into his head to kiss you or he might decide to take a piece out of you."

"I refuse to be a box lunch for any bear," Lenora announced firmly. "Go away, Mr. Bruin!"

The bear sat calmly where he was, his sleepy eyes fixed on Lenora, his pink tongue now and then licking his lips as if in anticipation.

"Where's a ranger?" Lenora demanded. "I want a ranger."

"We'll wait for you in the car," Shirley said as she and Beverly made their escape and settled down gleefully in the automobile to watch proceedings.

"Don't forget," Shirley called. "It is dangerous to feed the bears!"

"It isn't my idea—it's his!" Lenora retorted. "Go away, Mr. Bear!"

"We'll have to take a picture of this," Shirley giggled to Beverly, reaching into the back seat for Lenora's camera.

Unknown to her, they took several pictures of Lenora looking askance at the bear and trying to get past him to the car.

At last the bear, as if tired of waiting, shuffled to the side of the road, rose on his hind legs and proceeded to rub his back against a tree trunk, his front feet pawing the air while he scratched.

Lenora sprinted for the car and dived into the back

seat at the same moment Shirley started the motor.

"Saved by a flea!" Lenora sighed. "Do bears have fleas?"

"How should we know?" Beverly laughed. "Have you had enough of bears?"

"He would have made a beautiful rug," was Lenora's dreamy reply.

CHAPTER VI

San Francisco

THEY crossed from Oakland to San Francisco on the mighty bridge that spans the bay.

"Down there is the Golden Gate Bridge," Lenora said, proud of her knowledge.

"The Golden Gate!" Beverly echoed in awe.

"If I get any happier I'll burst," Shirley declared. "The Golden Gate! Remember when we were in college we used to dream of seeing all these places." She sighed with sheer delight. "Now—words fail me."

"I take it you are impressed," Lenora chuckled.

"Definitely so," Shirley agreed.

"San Francisco!" Lenora murmured. "City of the Seven Hills. Doesn't the mere name do something to you?"

"Fisherman's Wharf, Chinatown, Telegraph Hill," further elucidated Beverly. "'Frisco, here we come!"

"What shall we do first?" Shirley asked.

"Well," Lenora began ticking off things on her fingers, "when we go to Fisherman's Wharf I want to eat a lobster that has been cooked right before my eyes. When we go to Chinatown I want some genuine chop suey. Third, I want——"

"Food!" Shirley said in disgust. "Is that all you think about?"

"Most of the time," Lenora returned brightly.

When they turned off the bridge they drove up Market Street to see the shopping district.

Since they wanted to see and to do as much as possible in a very short space of time, they chose a hotel in the center of the city and immediately set about making arrangements for tours that would take them to all the points of interest. As they partially unpacked they talked over what to do first.

"I want to go to Chinatown," Lenora said. "I want to buy some souvenirs there."

"All right," Shirley agreed. "First, we'll have our lunch down at Fisherman's Wharf——"

"I've heard it is grand out at the Cliff House," Beverly offered.

"They must have restaurants in Chinatown," Lenora put in.

"It would be nice to ride through Golden Gate Park this afternoon and then see the Presidio where the soldiers live——"

"We might get in a little shopping in the stores, too," added Beverly.

"But I want to go to Chinatown!" Lenora persisted.

In the end it was all decided for them when they found an escorted tour leaving the hotel for a trip through Golden Gate Park to the Cliff House. Armed with cameras and a supply of films the girls boarded the bus.

"I can't believe it," Lenora sighed. "I just can't believe it! Me—in San Francisco! Do I look every inch the wide-eyed tourist?"

"It is hard to tell what you look like with dark glasses and all that camera stuff," Shirley returned laughingly.

The first stop the bus made was at the tiny Mission Dolores. White, with worn altars and pews, the little mission has stood proudly since 1776, triumphant over weather and earthquakes.

Over roads lined with palm trees the bus circled slowly through the rich greenness of Golden Gate Park. The girls' cameras were in constant use. Past the Japanese Pagoda and the famous windmills they came at last to the Cliff House, built on a wall of rock against which the Pacific Ocean beat a ceaseless rhythm. From the white house they could watch the seals sunning themselves on the rocks below.

"The blue Pacific!" Shirley sighed.

"Looks green to me," Lenora declared. "Are you sure they are live seals on those rocks?"

"Certainly they are," Beverly said. "Seal Rocks are famous."

"Then why doesn't somebody catch them and make coats out of them? There must be at least twelve or fifteen——"

"I wouldn't try it," Shirley advised with a laugh. "Come, let's buy some souvenirs. Time's a-wastin'."

The bus returned through the Presidio and on the return trip they had a much closer view of Golden Gate Bridge and Alcatraz. Back at the hotel they dressed for dinner, changed the films in their cameras and sallied forth again. They went to Fisherman's Wharf and ate in a small blue and white place where Lenora watched the chef cook the lobster she had ordered in a huge copper kettle on the sidewalk.

They took pictures of the fishing boats at anchor and then went on to Chinatown.

The buildings were ornate with their pagoda roofs and iron-grilled balconies. An odor of fragrant incense filled the air. Gaily colored lanterns strung along many of the streets shed a mellow glow and strange Oriental music came faintly to their ears. Smiling yellow faces and almond eyes peered from the interior of tiny shops. Many of the men were dressed in American-cut clothes while most of the women wore the long, brocaded gowns of the Orient.

In one building they entered there were tiers of balconies extending three floors above and two below the street floor. In the center, at the base of all the balconies, was a small pool of water fancifully entitled a Wishing Well from which the gods of fortune were supposed to look forth and grant any wisher his heart's desire for the receipt of a penny thrown into the green water.

"Come on, Beverly, make a wish," Lenora proposed. "I've made three already and I'd make some more if I had more pennies."

Shirley was consulting the sign hanging to one side of the well.

"It says you will get your heart's desire," she repeated. "Well, here goes." She tossed a penny into the green water and stared after it, wishing silently.

"I have my heart's desire," Beverly said with a smile. "I'll give you my pennies, Lenora, if you have so much to wish for."

"Aren't you going to make even one wish?"

"No."

"I wish I had everything I desire," Shirley sighed.

"That's tempting fate," Lenora declared. "However, I'll wish for you." She proceeded to do so while her friends looked on.

They passed store windows crowded with intricately carved work, butcher shops whose windows displayed dried frogs and eels and other delicacies. They peered into dark alleyways which they longed to explore but did not quite dare. They laughed at a Chinese puppet show. In the Tin How Temple they gazed in solemn awe at the ornately carved altar and had the meanings of some of the many prayer sticks explained to them. They were greatly impressed by the clock in the Western Union office which indicated the time of day in China. It was there that Lenora had the bright idea of sending Lois a telegram in Chinese. From there they went to the telephone exchange.

"Imagine," Lenora said in amazement, watching the operators at the switchboard, "those girls have to remember more than three thousand names because the subscribers don't have telephone numbers!"

"You would never get a job here with your memory," Shirley laughed.

The girls spent hours in Chinatown and it was late when they started back to the hotel. Despite the hour Lenora voiced a desire to go to the top of Telegraph Hill for a night view of the city and harbor. They took a cable car up Jones Street. By a slow, interesting, varied route, half of which they walked, they arrived at last at the high pinnacle overlooking the town. Breathless after the climb, the girls stood silent at the beauty of the lighted city at their feet. Battleships in the harbor stretched slender fingers of light up into the sky to form a crisscross pattern. A slender thread of yellow diamonds marked the Bay Bridge.

"What a climb!" Lenora managed at last. "It was worth it, though."

The wind from the sea blew against their faces and stirred the trees behind them.

"Let's sit here all night," Shirley proposed. "It is so romantic."

"And Roger in New York!" Lenora teased.

Beverly scarcely heard her friends' chatter. Here at her feet lay the city she had dreamed about so many times. All the magic of old stories seemed to reach up and engulf her now—stories of Barbary Coast, the old sailing ships, the great earthquake, robust, throbbing days of the early pioneers. Here was portrayed in brick and stone and electric lights courage and determination, loyalty and sacrifice. Here was a modern city, clean and firm, built on ruins of other cities; modern lives built on ghosts of other lives who had passed on courage and fortitude.

"Doesn't it do something to you?" Beverly asked the other girls, eyes shining. "San Francisco—at your feet!"

"I am impressed no end," Lenora said, "but I am also tired. Shall we go down?"

"You have no romance in your soul," Shirley declared. "You don't appreciate this."

"I do, too," Lenora retorted, "but at the moment I'd appreciate a bed more. We can come again. The view will still be here."

"The first time is always the best," Shirley said. "Besides, we go on to Los Angeles tomorrow."

"I'm coming back here," Beverly murmured. "I don't know when or how, but some day I'm coming back to San Francisco. Does that sound silly?"

"No," Shirley said, "and I'd like to come with you. We'll make it a promise, shall we?"

As the girls stood there talking, drinking in the scene below, a light blanket of fog began moving in from the sea until the lights were blurred and the outlines of buildings had melted into one dark shadow. Only then did they leave their post and return to the hotel.

CHAPTER VII

Lost

It was a sunny afternoon when they arrived in Los Angeles, having completed their long overnight drive from San Francisco via smooth highways bordered with tall pine and redwood trees. The streets of the city were crowded with shoppers and midafternoon traffic. On impulse they left the city proper and drove to Hollywood. Here there was almost as much traffic as there had been downtown but the girls scarcely saw it. They gazed about them eager for glimpses of famous spots and celebrities. In fact, so engrossed were they in looking about them that Shirley failed to step on the brake in time and her car rammed into the one ahead which had stopped for a traffic light.

Shirley alighted and the driver of the other car came back to meet her. They conferred for a moment over the locked bumpers, and then, with the help of a passer-by, the cars were separated without damage. The tall, handsome driver of the first car went on his way.

"What did he say? Weren't you thrilled to death? Did you get his autograph?" Lenora demanded in quick succession.

"Who?" Shirley asked blankly. "What are you talking about?"

"Didn't you recognize him?" Beverly asked.

"That was Gary Holden," Lenora informed her friend. "Simply the best-looking actor in town."

"Oh, was it?" Shirley asked as the car shot forward. "He was very nice about my bumping into him like that. From now on you can look at the scenery, but I'll keep my eyes on the road!"

"Look! There's the Brown Derby!"

"And Grauman's Chinese Theater."

"We have really arrived," Lenora sighed. "The door to Beverly's future! Behold!"

Beverly laughed. "Only perhaps."

"We shall see to it that you are famous," Lenora plotted. "We shall be your guiding angels, won't we, Shirley?"

"We shall see that she doesn't get into difficulties," Shirley agreed. "There's our hotel."

There was a letter from Larry waiting at the post office for Beverly when the girls called there. It had been written a week before when he and Mike arrived in South America. In it he promised to write again the next day when they returned from their intended flight into the interior. That letter should have been waiting, too, but it wasn't. Beverly was not alarmed, however. It might arrive at any moment. She gave the post office her address while in Los Angeles and went away confident that she would soon receive more mail from Larry.

Impatient to know what she was to do Beverly wasted no time in going to the studio that had purchased the movie rights to her book. Shirley and Lenora, eager to see what went on behind the scenes and how motion pictures were made, accompanied her. They got as far as the grilled iron gate where a uniformed employee stopped them.

Beverly told him who they wanted to see and that she

"Of course. You were in the back seat," he said. "Won't you sit down?" He indicated the chair opposite him.

"Oh, no, I couldn't," Lenora said. "I spoke to you because—ever since yesterday I've been trying to decide something."

"You don't want an autograph, surely!" he laughed.

Lenora laughed too. "No. I wanted to know—is your real name Percival Gerald Allen?"

"Sh-h-h!" He laughingly made a sign for silence. "I've been trying to live the Percival down. Please sit down, Miss——"

"Lenora Whitehill."

"Lenora——" he gazed at her in silence for a moment. "Not——"

"Yes. The girl whose bicycle you wrecked with your motorcycle."

"I always meant to come and see you after that accident, but I never quite had the courage," he chuckled.

"I probably would have scalped you if you had," she returned. "That bicycle was the pride and joy of my eleven years."

"What are you doing out here?" he asked. "Are you going into pictures?"

"Heavens, no!" Lenora laughed, and proceeded to tell him about the girls' trip west.

They had a delicious lunch and a very interesting visit before Shirley and Beverly found them.

The days went by swiftly. Beverly spent most of the day at the studio while Lenora and Shirley kept busy sightseeing and acquiring a suntan. They attended a gay première at one of the theaters on Hollywood Boulevard, and another time they went to a concert in the mammoth Hollywood Bowl. It was all very gay and interesting until one afternoon when Shirley returned from a shopping trip and found Lenora pacing nervously up and down.

"Where've you been?" Lenora greeted her.

"What's the matter?" Shirley asked calmly. "Gosh, it's hot. Sit down."

"Where's Beverly?" Lenora demanded next.

"Having a conference with Mr. Lloyd Phillips, the Third." Shirley dropped wearily into a chair and picked up a magazine to fan herself. "Will you please tell me what's wrong with you?"

Lenora thrust the newspaper she had been carrying at Shirley.

"Read that!" she commanded, indicating a small article at the bottom of the page.

"'Fliers lost in jungle,'" Shirley read aloud. "'Concern mounted today over the continued absence of two men who took off a week ago on a flight into the interior.'" She looked up mystified.

"Go on," Lenora urged.

"'Larry Owens was piloting the plane on a search to find friends of his companion, Michael McKay, who disappeared several months ago. According to plans confided to friends the two Americans were due to return to the airport days ago.'" Shirley stared at the newspaper, scarcely believing. "Lenora!"

"Do you suppose Beverly has seen it?" Lenora asked.

"No, I don't think so," Shirley replied. "She would have told us."

"How are we going to tell her?" Lenora asked.

"We shouldn't get alarmed," Shirley said wisely. "After all, that is an old newspaper. We don't want to worry Beverly unnecessarily. Larry might be safe now."

"Perhaps," Lenora agreed. "Still, she should know——"

"What should I know?" Beverly asked brightly from the doorway. "If it is something that will make me more angry I don't want to hear it. I have been blowing off steam all the way home. I don't see why they bought my book. The changes they propose to make would alter it so that even I wouldn't recognize it." She laughed. "Lenora, you enjoy a good argument. You should have been with me today." She dropped into a chair beside Shirley. "What have you two been doing? What were you talking about when I came in?"

"Um—uh—we came across an article in the paper," Lenora said uncomfortably.

"Did you receive another letter from Larry yet, Bev?" Shirley asked.

"No," Beverly replied. She sat up straighter. "Why? Is something wrong?"

Silently Shirley handed her the newspaper and then wandered to the window to stand beside Lenora.

"Larry's too good a flier to get lost in the jungle," Beverly's voice said behind them after a while.

"Of course," Lenora agreed promptly. "He is probably safe and sound now."

"That's last week's news," added Shirley.

They spoke cheerily, pushing back the doubts and fears that were in their hearts, not wanting to believe what they had read, yet knowing that fliers, even good ones, do get lost.

"You may get a letter tomorrow," Lenora continued brightly.

"Yes," agreed Beverly, but in her heart she wondered. She remembered the premonition she had had that morning when she stood and watched Larry's plane disappear in the clouds. It had been that same strange feeling that she had the last time they visited "White Corners." A sense of danger, of loss, yet nothing she could definitely name or see. Just a premonition of danger—of evil, and now—perhaps, it had come.

CHAPTER VIII

Beginning the Search

THE next day when there was no further news in the newspaper and Larry's long overdue letter was not forthcoming, Beverly wired the airport in South America. Their reply was brief and unsatisfactory, simply stating that nothing had been heard of the two fliers since they took off on their flight into the interior.

"I feel so helpless," Beverly said, pacing up and down, the wire in her hand. "He couldn't have vanished into thin air." She didn't dare put into words the dreadful picture she had of Larry lying injured in some fever-ridden swamp.

"I wonder what the jungle of South America is like," Lenora murmured from her cross-legged position at the foot of Shirley's chair.

"If there were only something we could do!" Shirley sighed.

"Do you suppose they have cannibals down there like they do in Africa?" Lenora asked and received a kick from Shirley.

Beverly stopped in her pacing, carefully folded the wire, and announced:

"I'm going down there."

"What?" Lenora leaped up. "But your book—the movie——"

"Larry is more important," Beverly said simply. "I'm going to the studio now and explain why I'm leaving."

"Beverly, don't you think you should wait and consider this carefully? What do you expect to do when you get there? It may all be a wild goose chase. Larry may turn up at any time. Lots of fliers get lost in the jungle. He may be on his way home this very minute——"

"And he may not," Beverly finished. "I have to know something definite. I can't sit here doing nothing, not even knowing if he is alive——" Her voice failed and she took a fresh grip on herself. "I hope you both will go on as if nothing had happened. I don't want to spoil your trip."

"Rubbish!" Lenora said briskly.

"Isn't there something we can do?" Shirley asked.

"No, thanks. I'll see you at dinner." Beverly picked up her hat and left.

The girls stared at each other thoughtfully.

"We could charter a plane," Lenora said at last.

"It would probably cost a fortune," Shirley frowned, "but we could see about it."

"Gary Holden owns a plane," Lenora continued.

"A lot of movie people do," was Shirley's reply.

"Do you suppose he would rent it to us?"

"Us?"

"Certainly. We can't let Beverly go down there by herself. Not now. I'm going along."

"I thought I'd go to New York and get Roger to take his boat down there," Shirley murmured.

"And we could all come home in it," Lenora finished. "A grand idea! Let's go and see Gary Holden."

"But, Lenora, he is practically a stranger," Shirley protested.

"He is not," Lenora denied. "I didn't say anything, but he went to school with me. Then he was plain Percival Gerald Allen. I promised I wouldn't spoil his glamour now by telling on him, but in a case like this——"

"What are we waiting for?" Shirley demanded.

When Beverly returned from the studio it was dinner-time, but neither Shirley nor Lenora was home, so she sat down to wait. The other girls came in a half-hour later full of tidings.

"Gary Holden is lending us his plane but, since he can't get away to pilot it himself, we'll have to hire a man who can bring the plane back," Lenora explained. "It shouldn't cost much just for that."

"Mr. Holden is going to get in touch with a pilot he knows and telephone us," added Shirley.

"When can I leave?" Beverly asked.

"Tomorrow, if you want to," Lenora said promptly.

The next morning when Beverly was ready to leave she found her friends' luggage piled with her own awaiting the taxi Shirley had telephoned for.

"But I thought——" Beverly began.

"That we would let you go alone?" Lenora demanded indignantly. "What do you think we are?"

"Lenora is going with you," Shirley explained. "I'm flying to New York to get Roger and his yacht. We'll meet you down there. And it is all decided," she finished firmly, as Beverly tried to speak, "so you needn't say a word."

"I'll be your chaperon," Lenora attempted to joke.

Beverly looked from one to the other, a film of tears in her eyes.

"It's good to have such friends."

"Shucks," Lenora said, swallowing a lump in her own throat. "There's the taxi."

They took off in the gray early morning hours. Since Shirley's plane would not leave until two hours later, she saw them off. The last glimpse they had of the airfield included her figure growing smaller and smaller as the plane soared higher into the sky. They flew all day with only a short stop at noon to refuel, and as the tropic night was rapidly darkening the sky, they came in sight of the airport.

Since it was past dinnertime when they had taxied from the airport to a hotel, they had a late meal served to them on the small balcony outside their room where they could watch the street traffic.

Afterward Beverly tried to telephone the field from

which Larry and Mike had taken off. Though she could hear the operator ringing, there was no response.

"It would be better to wait until morning," Lenora advised. "No one is working at this hour."

"I know," Beverly nodded, "but now that I am here I'm anxious to get things moving."

However, since the airport seemed the best place to start her search, Beverly was forced to spend the night in restless, uneasy waiting.

They rose early in the morning, breakfasted in the hotel, and then taxied out to the airfield. Beverly found herself looking eagerly for a glimpse of the sturdy little *Red Bird III,* hoping Larry and Mike had returned safely, but there was only a yellow biplane standing idle before an empty hangar.

The office of the manager of the field was in a small building and was divided into two rooms by a thin partition. The girls, waiting in the outer room, could hear clearly the conversation in the next one. At first it was in smooth, Spanish-tinged English, but then there came the firm, clear tones of a North American voice.

"But something must be done, Rodriguez," it announced distinctly. "They must be found, do you understand?"

"That voice!" Beverly murmured.

"Sh-h-h," Lenora warned, quite frankly eavesdropping.

"He is your friend, no?" the Spanish voice was asking.

"He is my friend, yes," came the reply. "As you are."

"Ah, but I am your live friend," was the jesting answer.

"You think they are not alive?"

The girls could not see the characteristic shrug of the Spaniard's shoulders, but they could sense the gesture accompanying his words.

"It is two weeks they are gone. Where are they, Señor? No message has come from them in all that time. Many things might happen—no petrol, a crash——"

"Lenora!"

"Steady!" Lenora caught Beverly's hand in hers. "They may not be talking about Larry."

"They are, I know it! That voice—it is so like——" she broke off as the other person in the adjoining room spoke again.

"In your report you say you had some of your men out searching."

"Sí, that is so."

"What did they do? How far did they go?"

"They have made flights over the mountains into the

interior—the same route Señor Owens was to take. They could find nothing."

"Did you have ground parties cover the route?"

"Señor, it is impossible. There are many mountains, plains, jungle—even unfriendly tribes in the interior. We could see no wreckage from the air. Therefore, we did not think——"

"You will have a plane and pilot ready this afternoon to take me over the same route they were to fly," was the crisp command.

"Sí, but I am afraid it is useless. Was he your very good friend, Señor?"

"He was. Remember, Rodriguez! At one o'clock."

"Sí. It will be waiting."

The door opened and from the inner office emerged a tall individual whose white linen suit accentuated the dark brown of his skin. He merely glanced at the girls waiting and then, at the door, turned back and stared in frank disbelief.

"Beverly! Lenora!"

"Jim!"

"It isn't possible," he said. "I'm dreaming."

"No." Lenora pinched his arm. "We're real. See?"

He put an arm about each of them. "Why didn't you let me know? What are you doing here?"

"Larry," Beverly said simply.

"I know," Jim agreed. "But don't worry too much. He will come out all right. We might hear from him any moment."

Somehow the sight of Jim, big and bronzed and smiling, made the loss of Larry so much more painful.

"Your friend didn't think so," Beverly nodded toward the other room. "He seems to think——"

"Rodriguez?" Jim laughed. "He is a lazy good-for-nothing who is getting too fat to leave his desk. He doesn't know Larry or," his eyes smiled down at her, "what he has to come back to."

"I heard you ask for a plane to fly the route Larry and Mike took. I want to go with you, Jim."

"Okay. But how about some lunch first? We'll go to the American Club."

Lenora saw he was deliberately being light and cheerful for Beverly's benefit and she came to his aid.

"We haven't been initiated into South American dishes yet," she said. "Tell me, do they actually eat grasshoppers?"

"I don't think you'll find them on the menu at the American Club," he laughed. "It is so long since I've had someone from home to talk to I shall probably keep you busy for hours answering my questions."

The dining room of the club to which Jim took them was light and cool. Flowers graced every table and from behind vine-covered latticework an orchestra provided faint, mellow music. The food was delicious and, though Beverly scarcely touched hers, Lenora was loud in her praise of it. It was Lenora, too, who answered most of Jim's questions about home and told him about Shirley and Roger's plan to bring the *Susabella* to South America to aid in the search for Larry.

"Jim, it is almost one o'clock," Beverly said at last. "Don't you think we had better go? The plane will be waiting——"

"Yes," Jim agreed. "I'm sorry, Lenora. The largest plane Rodriguez has is a three passenger, and with Beverly and the pilot and me——"

"I hadn't planned on going," Lenora said cheerfully. "I have some letters to write. I'll meet you at the hotel tonight."

The airport loomed as a small brown patch surrounded by lush green growth, increasing in size as their plane approached until they could clearly distinguish buildings and parked cars.

They had been up for hours, flying hundreds of miles over dark-green fertile land, high barren hills, and plains dotted here and there with small thatched hut villages. There had been no sign of the fallen *Red Bird;* no indication of any wreck had broken the expanse of jungle lying beneath them. Everything had been tranquil and undisturbed. If Larry's plane had fallen, all trace of it had been immediately swallowed up.

The plane rolled to a stop. Jim opened the door of the tiny cabin and jumped out, turning to help Beverly. They said good-bye to their smiling pilot; thanked Rodriguez and climbed into Jim's car. Then Beverly gave the first indication of tears. She bowed her head in her hands and a little choked sob escaped her. Jim put his arms around her and let her cry on his shoulder.

"I'm sorry," she said at last, drawing away. "It is the first time I've done that."

"It sometimes helps to cry it out," Jim said, starting the car.

"It's just that it seems so hopeless."

"Ever hear the saying 'No news is good news'?" he asked. "We've got to believe that now."

Jim halted the car at the edge of a bluff overlooking the ocean below. The sun had set and twilight was spreading a purple veil over the world.

"Peaceful up here, isn't it?" Jim sighed. "I come here whenever anything is troubling me or my world seems topsy-turvy."

"Isn't there anything we can do, Jim?" Beverly asked. "You know the country down here, its customs and people. What could have happened to him?"

"Quite obviously his plane is down somewhere," Jim said seriously. "Perhaps he got off his course—he may be lost in the mountains. In that case it might be weeks before he could get a message out. If he is down in the jungle——"

"We've got to do something," Beverly continued. "You spoke of a searching party this morning to Rodriguez. What did you have in mind?"

"Oh, a trip on foot or mule over the route they were flying. You saw yourself how difficult it is to sight anything from the air."

"How long would it take?" Beverly asked.

"That is difficult to say. It would depend on a lot of things—the route, the weather, what obstacles we found—say, a month maybe."

"When could we start?"

"Wait a minute! You mean, you want to make such a trip?"

"Of course."

"Oh, now, Beverly, look here. It would be dangerous and tiresome enough for me or Roger and it is no place for you."

"Nevertheless, I'm going," was her firm rejoinder. "If you won't take me I'll hire another guide."

"And get properly lost," Jim agreed. "For months I worked through jungle and swampland. I guess I know it as well as anyone, and I'm telling you it is no place for a girl. Suppose you let me go——"

"While I sit here and worry?" Beverly smiled. "You know I never liked to wait, Jim. I'm going with you. If you find Larry I want to be there."

CHAPTER IX

The Fallen Red Bird

"You mean we're all going?" Lenora demanded gleefully. "We are going to sail the *Susabella* right up the river and surprise all the animals and natives and things?"

"If you want to," Beverly said. "The river isn't deep enough to bring the *Susabella* all the way in but Roger will bring it as far as he can. There we'll meet them and take to small boats—native canoes I guess you'd call them."

"I can hardly wait," Lenora declared. "I should get some marvelous pictures. Maybe I could do a series on the life of the natives. That's an idea. I'll work on it."

Two days later an air mail letter came from Shirley with the news that the *Susabella* had sailed from New York and was on its way to South America. On board were Shirley, Roger, Larry's brother, David, and, of course, the boat's crew. They would enter the Amazon River at its mouth in the Atlantic and sail as far inland as possible. Beverly would hear later where to meet them.

At best, given excellent weather conditions and tides, it would be days before Beverly could expect to hear from those aboard the yacht. Meanwhile there were preparations to make for the trip into the interior. She had not realized the details such a journey entailed until she accompanied Jim on his errands. There were guides to be hired, purchases to be made of supplies and clothing suitable for such a trip. Without Jim the girls would have been at a loss. They would never have thought of all the things needed.

Despite her impatience and anxiety Beverly could see the wisdom of sound preparations for their expedition. There was no telling what they would find so it was best to be prepared for all emergencies. No word came from Larry and Mike, but Beverly refused to give up hope. Her friends could not help but admire her persistence and courage. If they themselves had any doubts about Larry's survival they did not voice them in Beverly's presence, but pretended confidence in a happy ending to their search.

At last came a wireless message from Shirley. The *Susabella* was progressing inland. It was time for Beverly, Jim, Lenora, and their guide to start.

It was a dreary morning when they finally began their trip. The sky was overcast and the air was hot and sticky. They traveled the first day in automobiles. The morning of the second day they deserted the cars for the donkeys they would ride part of the way.

"I don't know," Lenora said, eyeing the little gray beast as he stood docile under the guide's hand, waiting for his rider. "I've never ridden a donkey before. I've heard they are stubborn critters."

"Elmer is gentle like a lamb, Señorita," the guide, Manuel, assured her smilingly.

Doubtfully, Lenora got into the saddle. Elmer stood quietly. In fact he stood so quietly he refused to start with the rest of the party.

"Come on, Elmer. Get going. Be a nice boy," Lenora coaxed.

Elmer stood as though glued to the spot, blinking his eyes sleepily.

"Maybe he thinks *I* should carry *him,"* Lenora said at last.

"I don't understand," Manuel declared, distressed.

"Perhaps if we build a fire under him," Lenora suggested helpfully.

"I think, Señorita, it is your yellow hat," Manuel said meekly.

"Take it off, Lenora, so we can get started," Jim said.

"You would buy a yellow one!" Beverly laughed.

"I will not take it off," Lenora retorted indignantly. "He can't see it. Why should he care what I wear?"

"Elmer is very sensitive," Manuel pleaded. "He does not like the yellow color, Señorita."

"Of all the screwy ideas," Lenora grumbled. "Oh, very well." She removed the hat and handed it to Manuel who waved it in front of Elmer, pouring a torrent of Portuguese upon the little donkey.

Elmer shook his head and took a few dainty steps forward. He obediently trotted after the guide's pony when the party started.

"What next?" Lenora wanted to know. "A donkey that

objects to yellow hats! Well, now I have seen everything."

They rode steadily all day, and dismounted at nightfall, stiff and tired. They were up again early the next morning and by noon had reached a small, busy town in the harbor of which lay the white *Susabella,* flag flying, her brass polished and shining in the sun. Shirley and Roger were leaning over the rail.

"It is almost as if you had brought a breath of New York with you," Lenora declared, hugging Shirley. "How are they managing without us?"

"They are holding up as well as can be expected," Roger smiled.

"Hello, everybody!" David Owens came from the companionway.

The others felt it was a dramatic moment—this meeting of Larry's fiancée and his brother.

"One of us should burst into tears," David said smilingly to Beverly, holding her at arms' length.

"Why?" Beverly asked swiftly. "If we thought the search was hopeless we wouldn't be here."

"That's the spirit!" David declared admiringly. "Keep your chin up, Bev. We'll find him if we have to rip up the jungle tree by tree!"

"As a start we might get our luggage off the boat and be on our way," Roger suggested.

It was an adventure even if it had a grave purpose. This trek into the interior could not fail to be exciting and thrilling even as they sought vainly for some sign, some trace of the two men who had vanished.

Jungle, deep and impenetrable, swallowed them as they left the *Susabella* in safe harbor and took to small, sturdy canoes. Their boats moved rapidly and noiselessly with the current.

Each canoe carried three people. The first held Manuel, his aide, and all the food supplies. In the second canoe were Beverly, David, and Jim. The third held Shirley, Lenora, and Roger; and in the last canoe was a small, smiling native, guardian over the rest of their luggage.

According to their map, Larry and Mike had flown nearly all the way over the river. Therefore, their friends had high hopes that by following the same river they would find some sign of the missing fliers.

They covered several miles that afternoon, leaving civilization farther and farther behind. When the sun began to sink beyond the trees Manuel headed toward the shore to camp for the night.

They retired early after a good dinner but Beverly lay wakeful. It seemed so hopeless to search through this dense green growth. She thought of White Corners as she had last seen it, shining in the setting sun, so safe and secure. It was there, as Larry had said it would be, waiting for them.

"Nothing shall ever part us, Beverly. I promise you." Larry had said that, too. He had been so confident that they would be together always. And now——

Morning was alive with bird cries and red sunlight on the river. The party took to the canoes again and set off on another leg of their tedious journey. The glare of the hot sun was intense and their eyes ached from constant watching, striving to penetrate the thick undergrowth on the riverbanks for some sign of the fallen *Red Bird*.

They ate their midday lunch from boxes that had been prepared early that morning, not wanting to take the time to camp and cook a meal. Bird calls drifted sweetly to their ears. Foliage on the riverbanks stirred as startled animals fled from sight. Now and then huge shadows in the water moved from the path of their boats.

"I will be so glad to see Broadway again I'll never want to leave it," Lenora declared.

"You're not homesick!" Shirley smiled.

"Who says I'm not?" Lenora demanded. "I am so homesick I—hello! What's up?"

Beverly, in the boat ahead, was motioning in toward shore, talking swiftly to Jim and David. Their canoe turned toward the riverbank and the others followed.

"What is it?" Lenora called, scrambling from the boat in such haste she stepped knee-deep into water.

"Beverly saw something," Jim said, hastily snatching up his rifle to follow Beverly and David who were disappearing into the jungle.

Eager to end their search, yet almost afraid of what they might find, Beverly and David made as much haste as the tangled vines and jungle growth would permit. They burst suddenly into a small clearing and stopped, struck dumb by what they saw.

Its glory gone, the proud wings crumpled, the gleaming silver propeller a twisted fragment of steel, the *Red Bird III* lay silent and deserted. The red fuselage caught between two gnarled trees, the tail suspended over a branch, the wings crippled, it was hard to believe this was the same plane she had stood and watched mount gallantly into the clouds.

"Larry!" Beverly whispered.

"Wait," said David and moved forward.

He had to crawl on hands and knees to see into the upside-down cockpit. Once or twice he said Larry's name aloud. But it was no use. The *Red Bird* was empty, the secret of its occupants locked within its twisted frame.

"Beverly! David!" The others were lost and shouting.

"Here!" David called.

"What did you find?" Shirley asked eagerly. "Oh!"

"The *Red Bird!"* Lenora gasped.

There was a sudden silence as they gazed upon the fallen airship. Day after day they had hoped for the end of their search. Even in their wildest thoughts and fears they had retained a glimmer of hope. Now it was gone. This was the end of the trail.

Roger and Jim took charge and assigned tasks to each one as they planned to camp at the spot. Tents were put up. A fire was started and a meal prepared. But no one had any appetite. They tried to eat but the silence was heavy. Over them was the shadow of the *Red Bird* and the loss of their comrades.

Lenora emerged from the girls' tent and sat down beside Shirley on a fallen tree trunk.

"Where's Beverly?"

"She said she was going for a little walk," Shirley replied.

"Alone?"

"She said she wanted to think," Shirley continued in a worried tone.

Lenora was silent for a moment. Then:

"Shirley, do you suppose—I mean, I wonder if—could Larry and Mike have been killed in the plane crash?"

Shirley dug viciously at the ground with the stick she held.

"I suppose they could have," she said at last. "But there is no proof that they were."

"The jungle is such a dangerous place anything could happen," Lenora shivered. "Poor Beverly."

"Bev is braver than I could be," Shirley declared bluntly. "I'd probably be tearing my hair."

"It is as if her feelings were frozen," Lenora continued thoughtfully. "It scares me a little that she can be so controlled."

"Until this afternoon when we found the plane she refused to believe that Larry was really lost. Now it is almost hopeless."

"What's hopeless?" Jim asked, coming up behind them. "Where's Beverly?"

"She went for a walk," Lenora replied.

"She shouldn't be alone out here," Jim said and strode off in search of the girl.

He came upon Beverly sitting at the base of a gnarled, twisted tree, tossing broken twigs into the river to watch them float downstream.

"Hi, there!" He seated himself beside her.

"Jim, do you think Larry was—killed when the *Red Bird* crashed?"

The directness and unexpectedness of her question took him aback.

"No, I don't think so," he said at last slowly.

"Why don't you think so?" she asked, her eyes intent upon his face.

"Well, for one thing, we found no trace of either Larry or Mike. If they had been killed in the plane I should think there would be some sign——"

"I think so, too," Beverly nodded. "It is the only thing I can think."

"The question is," Jim continued with a frown, "what do we do now? This looks like the end of the trail."

"I've been thinking of that, too," she agreed. "They've left no trail that we could follow. Therefore, the only thing for us to do is to go to their destination. Perhaps we'll find them there."

"And just what was their destination?" Jim asked. "They were looking for two men, weren't they? In that case they might be anywhere in South America."

"The two men whom Larry was seeking came to find an emerald," Beverly said. "No one knows whether they did or not. Perhaps their trail led Larry and Mike to the emerald and if we find the stone we may find them."

"It sounds so simple—put like that," Jim said, "but do you realize what it involves? South America is a big place. How can we find one emerald?"

"I'm looking for Larry," Beverly said, "and if the emerald can lead me to him then we've got to find it!"

"But where will we start?" Jim wanted to know. "Did Larry tell you any of his plans?"

"He told me a little about them," Beverly said, "but he didn't know exactly where the emerald was. I believe it is connected with some of the native religious rites."

"That's bad," Jim said frankly. "We don't want any fuss with the native tribes."

"In all the time you worked down here, didn't you hear any stories about a fabulous emerald?"

"None," he confessed promptly.

"Manuel!" Beverly said. "He might know."

"I'll get him." Jim scrambled to his feet and disappeared among the trees. He was back in a moment with their smiling, soft-spoken guide.

"Manuel, have you lived in South America all your life?" Jim asked.

"I was born in Mexico," Manuel said. "I came here with my family when I was ten, Señor."

"Have you ever heard any stories about an emerald, Manuel?" Jim continued.

"An emerald, Señor?" their guide murmured slowly.

"It might be in a native temple——" Beverly began.

"Sí," Manuel nodded quickly. "I have heard of it."

"You have?" Jim pounced upon him. "Where is it?"

"It is not good to know, Señor."

"What have you heard about it, Manuel?" Beverly asked.

"It is evil to even speak of it, Señorita," Manuel said in

a whisper. "It glows with fire and has the power of evil within it. It is cursed with the curse of a thousand years."

"Tommyrot!" Jim said crisply. "The natives are a superstitious lot. They believe anything you tell them."

"It is truly evil, Señor," Manuel assured him. "Many people have sought it but none have returned from their search."

"Manuel, this is the twentieth century. We don't believe in witches and goblins—or curses," Jim said firmly. "We want to see the emerald and you must take us there."

"No, Señor," Manuel said promptly.

"You will be well paid," Jim assured him.

"Anything you want, Manuel," added Beverly.

"Even so, I cannot," Manuel declared. "Do not go, Señor. It is evil."

"We must go," Beverly interrupted. "Jim, if Larry and Mike heard this story they would be sure to go."

"Probably," Jim nodded. "Manuel, you must take us to this place."

But Manuel was not to be swayed. He refused to be lured into guiding them in their search. Obviously he was terrified by the stories he had heard about the curse upon the stone. At last, however, he agreed to guide them part of the way and show them the route they must follow to reach their goal.

Beverly felt more hopeful when she went to sleep that night. The story of the emerald was just the sort of adventure that would appeal to Larry and Mike. She felt sure that if she and the others succeeded in reaching the famous stone they would find Larry.

CHAPTER X

A Discovery

"I," LENORA announced to the world in general, "am disgusted. Mosquitoes and heat and snakes and more mosquitoes!"

"You wouldn't go back to the *Susabella* as we wanted you to," David reminded her with a grin.

"And miss all the fun?" Lenora demanded. "If anyone finds an emerald I want to be there."

The morning after Jim's and Beverly's talk with Manuel the group had held a council of war around the breakfast table. The situation had been presented to the others frankly, with all Manuel's fears and superstitions. The dangers had been plainly voiced and then the young men tried to persuade the girls to return to the *Susabella* to wait. The suggestion had been promptly and loudly rejected. This search, the girls declared, had been their idea in the very beginning and they did not intend to stop now.

Camp was broken and much of their equipment was stored in their canoes, which, in turn, were hidden along the riverbank. From now on they would not be able to travel in boats but would have to make their way on foot through the jungle. It was much harder going and their evening camps were not as comfortable, since they had been forced to leave much of their equipment behind.

It was their second day of walking when Lenora made her announcement. Progress was slow and difficult. At first it had been interesting, this walk through an environment so different from what they were used to, but they soon became weary and the jungle lost its enchantment.

Manuel persistently tried to persuade them to give up this search, but the more he protested, the more determined they became.

The animal life they saw made their journey more interesting and gave Lenora subjects for her pictures. Monkeys chattered at them from high tree branches and once they came upon a pair of zebra drinking at a deep, still forest pool.

"I'll bet Beverly's next book will be about the jungle," David declared with a laugh. "The Autobiography of a Chimpanzee."

"With illustrations by Madame Lenora," added Shirley.

"We will tell all," Lenora declared dramatically. "We will—David! Look out!"

At her scream David jumped aside just as there came a dreaded hissing sound and something slithered over the toe of his boot.

"I will never be the same," Shirley declared. "I'll have heart failure if snakes don't stop popping out at me."

"In New York taxis do the same thing when you want to cross the street," Lenora said with a shrug.

"I'll take the taxis," Shirley retorted promptly.

"I'm hungry," Lenora announced. "Isn't it lunchtime?"

"How about it, Manuel? Is this a good spot to stop and eat?" Jim asked their guide.

"A little more, Señor," Manuel replied.

The guide found a cool spot near fresh water and they sat down gratefully to rest and eat.

When their lunch had disappeared and they felt rested they again made preparations to continue their journey. They were about to start when Manuel approached Jim and announced:

"Manuel will leave you, Señor."

"You mean this is as far as you go?" Jim asked. "You won't take us the rest of the way?"

"I urge you, Señor, do not go farther. Forget the jewel. You cannot hope to possess it."

"If you leave us, Manuel, we will be lost in the jungle," Lenora put in fearfully.

In spite of their pleadings, Manuel remained firm in his decision. They had come to the parting of the ways and Manuel was going back to safety. Sadly the group watched the slender figure of their guide disappear down the path they had come.

"A fine thing!" Lenora declared. "Our guide walks out on us. Now what will happen?"

"Manuel is doing what he believes is best," Jim murmured. "It isn't too late for those who want to go with him."

There was silence and then Jim slung his pack on his shoulder.

"Okay. Let's go."

They moved off after him feeling that they had taken a decisive and important step in their determination to continue. Almost anything might lie ahead of them. The very thought filled them with keen alertness and a spirit of adventure.

Their camp that night seemed lost and uncertain without Manuel's expert knowledge and guidance to smooth difficulties and right mistakes. The young people sat around their campfire and tried to tell stories and sing songs, bravely striving to maintain a cheerful front. Yet in the heart of each one was an awareness of the jungle growth around them. Black, impenetrable silence surrounded them on all sides. Even the friendly light of the stars overhead was blotted out. Mysterious, uncanny whispers came from the shadows and at last they decided to go to sleep to forget their surroundings.

Morning light brought them renewed hope and confidence, and they set out jauntily on the route Manuel had advised. Today, perhaps, they would reach their goal. They sang as they marched along, rousing monkeys in the trees to furious chatter and startling the brilliant-plumaged birds that flew across their path.

"I think I'll start a Back-To-Nature movement," Lenora declared. "Nature is wonderful."

"Yes, isn't it?" Roger agreed, slapping at a mosquito.

"From Yellowstone Park to the wilds of South America in only a few weeks," continued Lenora. "How we do get around!"

Beverly and Jim, in the lead, stopped suddenly and Beverly pointed to the foothills they had been steadily approaching all day. She had been studying the formations through Jim's field glasses.

"The holes in the rock look almost like doors and windows," she declared.

Jim studied them in silence for a moment.

"It might be the remains of an ancient stone village."

"Cliff dwellers here?" David asked.

"Could it be part of the ancient Inca kingdom?" Shirley wanted to know.

Jim laughed. "I wouldn't know. My knowledge of native history is very poor, but I do know that some native villages did exist in this part of the country. They still do for that matter. In ancient times they were everything from sun worshippers to head-hunters."

"Cheerful news," Lenora said dryly.

"What was the last census on the head-hunters?" Roger laughed. "Are they still active?"

Jim frowned. "I have heard that there are one or two remote tribes. In fact, about ten months ago I met a man who had barely escaped with his life from a tribe that still practices the art of shrinking human heads until they are no larger than dolls' heads. I don't know what section of the country they inhabit."

"Maybe we are walking right into some of them," Lenora said with a fearful glance over her shoulder.

"Don't be silly," Shirley directed nervously. "We haven't seen a single sign of life. If there had been a village we would have seen it."

"Let's go on," David proposed eagerly. "I suggest we go and examine those stones more closely and see if it really is an abandoned village."

"You think of the nicest things," Lenora grumbled.

"Maybe we'll discover a lost civilization and become famous," David told her brightly.

"I'd rather discover a short cut to Times Square," Lenora replied.

"I thought you were an adventurous soul," Roger teased.

"Manuel took my adventurous spirit with him," Lenora said glumly. "Right now I can smell danger and I don't like it."

They resumed their journey, walking more swiftly now. It was a good distance to the rocky foothills. By the time they reached there the sun was well started on its descent in the western sky.

Roger and David eagerly climbed up into the first cave-like room. They reappeared later, each brandishing an ancient stone club.

"Come on up," Roger shouted. "There's a whole village here to be discovered."

The others clambered up until all of them were engaged in exploring the caves and crevices among the rocks.

"I have the strangest feeling that someone is watching us," Lenora confided to Beverly as they stooped to enter a small room through a low doorway.

"We are the only ones here," Beverly returned with a smile.

The room into which they had stepped was cool and shadowed and barren. There was not so much as a stone in it.

"Lenora! Look here!" Beverly dropped to one knee in the center of the floor and looked around.

"What is it?"

"Footprints," Beverly said. "Hundreds of them."

In the dust on the floor were countless impressions made at a former time by absent, unknown inhabiters of the house.

"There's another doorway. Let's see where it leads," Lenora suggested, unimpressed with Beverly's discovery.

They had to bend almost in half to pass through the tiny doorway into the inner room. The moment they stood upright they saw it. Rays from the setting sun entered through a small square opening in the roof and fell directly upon a large, crudely cut stone figure standing against one wall in whose cupped hands lay a dark stone, the heart of which seemed aglow with fire.

"Jeepers creepers!" Lenora whistled. "Look at the size of the thing! It must be worth millions."

It was the emerald they sought! Here at last was proof of all the fantastic stories they had heard.

"I don't see why Manuel was so scared," Lenora continued. "It is only a stone statue."

"Why hasn't someone taken it before this?" Beverly

asked softly. "There must be something more, Lenora. It couldn't be this simple."

"What else is there?" Lenora demanded. "Here we are. There is the emerald. What's to prevent our taking it?"

"Those footprints, perhaps. I didn't like them," Beverly told her with a frown. "Let's get the others and show them the stone."

"All right," Lenora agreed, "but why can't we take the stone out to them?"

Beverly led the way out into the sunlight. Their friends were descending from the rocks when Lenora called to them.

"Hi, there! We've found it. The emerald is here—as big as a duck egg."

Their friends seemed to stand spellbound. Then Jim began running toward them shouting, gesticulating excitedly. It took Beverly and Lenora a moment to realize that what he was so excited about was behind them. They turned, but it was too late to escape. The rocks were suddenly swarming with shouting, painted, brown-skinned natives.

CHAPTER XI

Captives

BEVERLY stood at the door of a small thatched hut in which the three girls were held captive and stared between the bamboo poles that barricaded the entrance. There was a semicircle of huts similar to theirs and at one end of the cleared space in front of the small houses was a much larger hut, decorated lavishly with dried white bones and small shrunken heads.

"It is odd," Beverly murmured. "They brought us here and they made sure that we can't escape, yet they haven't made any attempt to harm us."

"They act as if now that they have us they don't know

she stood in the hot sun and waited for their next move.

At last the witch doctor raised the spear he carried and gave a loud, hoarse shout that was bloodcurdling in its weirdness. Then he turned and ran lightly to the mysterious hut into which Beverly had sought admittance. At the doorway he stood with folded arms, his beady black eyes watching her, waiting. What was to happen now?

Evidently the next move was up to her so she walked slowly across the clearing, stopping once to look back at Shirley and Lenora and then at the other hut where Jim, David, and Roger were crowded at the door, all watching her. Jim raised a hand in silent salute and as she waved in return she thought how like a last farewell it was.

She glanced at the witch doctor. There was almost a smirk on his face. Did he think she was afraid to pass him? She raised her head and stepped into the cool darkness of the hut. The sudden transition from bright sunlight to soft shadows was blinding for a moment. Then she made out a figure seated at the rear of the small room.

"Am I dreamin'?" A voice demanded. A vibrant, Irish voice!

"Mike?" Beverly ventured.

"It is and I'm seein' an angel! What are you doing here? Don't tell me these brown devils have taken over New York!"

"We came here looking for you and Larry," Beverly replied, moving toward the sound of his voice. Mike was sitting on a bed of dried grass, one ankle bandaged with torn bits of cloth. He started to rise but Beverly motioned him back.

"Where is he, Mike?"

"I wish I knew," Mike said drearily. "You shouldn't be here, Beverly. You must try to get away the first chance you have."

"What happened, Mike?" Beverly asked. "We saw the wreck of the *Red Bird*."

"Ah, and a beautiful wreck it was, too," Mike said, shaking his head sadly. "The trees smashed our plane as if it were made of paper."

"You weren't hurt?" Beverly murmured.

"No, not then," Mike replied. "We started out to walk to the nearest village. We came upon that cursed emerald in the stone temple where these fellows worship their pagan gods. We were about to help ourselves to the stone when the natives rushed in. There was a beautiful fight.

I fell off the rocks and sprained my ankle. Larry disappeared and I haven't seen him since."

Beverly was silent. Another disappointment! The sight of Mike had raised her hopes. She had felt so sure that at last their search was ended. Now they were up against another stone wall. What could have happened to Larry?

"You're sure he isn't in one of the other huts?" Beverly asked.

"No, he isn't," Mike said soberly. "I was the only one they brought back. What they are saving me for I don't know."

"Do you think he could have escaped?" Beverly persisted.

"Perhaps he did," Mike nodded. "There is another village, a friendly one, about five miles west of here. That is where we were going when we came across the emerald. Even so, if Larry did escape and went there for help, he has had plenty of time to come back here."

"Unless he got lost," Beverly said. "How long has it been, Mike?"

"This is the third day."

Three days! Three eternities! Three empty voids of time in which anything might have happened.

"Where is this village?" Beverly asked. "Tell me how to get there."

"You couldn't do it," Mike returned at once. "It is all jungle."

"Tell me," Beverly said firmly. "Someone has to go for help."

Mike seized a thin stick and drew a small square on the dirt floor. "Here is this village and over here, directly west, is the other village. To reach it one has to go around here, avoiding the swampland, through the jungle. There is a medical missionary there who would help us." It was only a vague diagram in the dust but later Beverly was glad she had studied it so carefully.

"Looks as if my visiting time is up," Beverly smiled.

There was a scuffling noise at the door and the witch doctor, his feathers shivering, strode in. He gesticulated to Beverly and seizing her arm started toward the door.

"I'll try and get him to let me come back later," she called over her shoulder.

Lenora and Shirley pounced on her the minute she was inside the familiar hut.

"What did you see? What was over there?" Lenora demanded. "It took you so long——"

"Sit down," Shirley advised. "You look as though you had seen a ghost."

Beverly nodded.

"For goodness' sake, what was it?"

"Mike."

"You mean——" Lenora stared in openmouthed wonder.

"Over there?" Shirley finished.

"Bev, are you sure you feel all right?" Lenora insisted.

"Of course I'm all right," Beverly said. "I saw him, I tell you. Mike is over there."

Lenora let out a yell that should have made her a star member of the cannibal choir.

"And Larry——" Shirley ventured.

"Mike doesn't know," Beverly said drearily. "He must be lost in the jungle—somewhere."

CHAPTER XII

Beverly's Plan

STANDING at the doorway Beverly stared across the clearing to the hut Mike occupied. It was hours later. The witch doctor had entered Mike's hut once and had come out alarmingly fast, followed by an earthen jug that narrowly missed his head. There had been a hurried council and now there was the insistent beating of a ceremonial drum. It had gone on for hours and it could mean only one thing: the natives were preparing for some kind of action.

"If only that noise would stop!" Lenora groaned, pressing both hands over her ears.

"Something is going to happen," Shirley said ominously. "I felt it. Did either of you notice—will it be a full moon tonight?"

"Tomorrow night," Beverly replied.

"Trust an engaged girl to know the status of the moon," Lenora giggled. "What difference does it make?"

"Yes," Beverly agreed. "Why do you ask?"

"That must be what they are waiting for," Shirley mused. "In that book I read it said that some of the native tribes make sacrifices to their gods when the moon is full."

There was a moment of thoughtful silence, then Beverly shook the bars of their prison in angry impatience. "I've got to get out of here!"

"To go where?" Lenora asked dryly.

"To get help," Beverly retorted. "Mike told me how to reach the next village. I've got to get there."

"How?"

"We could dig a tunnel," Lenora offered.

"This is no time for jokes," Shirley said sternly.

Beverly turned to the doorway and screamed at the top of her voice.

"That ought to bring some attention," she declared.

Something had to be done. They had to get help and get it swiftly. The missionary was their only hope and it was up to her to reach him.

"It's funny when you think of it," Lenora said. "Larry and Mike came to rescue someone. We came to rescue them, and now somebody has to rescue us. It is a vicious circle. There will be enough of us here after a while to work from the inside."

"Work from the inside," Beverly murmured. "I wonder."

Beverly went to the doorway of their little house and looked out. Several of the young warriors were standing before the chief's hut. Beverly's scream had attracted the witch doctor and several other warriors, and the group came to the girls' door. Beverly repeated the pantomime she had used that morning and finally the witch doctor signaled that she was to be brought out. When the door was opened Beverly strode bravely out into their midst. They must not guess that her knees were shaking or how much she wanted to turn and run.

A heavy silence had fallen over the village. Beverly had a fleeting glimpse of anxious faces peering from the open doorways of the huts. Women had stopped their work to watch and the children had paused in their play to turn bright, curious eyes upon her.

She carefully considered each warrior in the group, slowly turning her glance from one to the other until she chose the youngest man there. He was scarcely older than she and the trophies he wore, results of his prowess on the hunt, were new. She put out a hand and touched the small skull he wore on a cord about his neck. Hastily the man backed away. A jabbering broke out among the others and then a heavy, ominous silence settled again as they watched her.

Beverly glanced down at her wrist. She wore three narrow silver bracelets. One of these she removed and held out to the young warrior. After a moment of hesitation he stepped forward and took it. Then he retreated to the midst of his companions and they considered the bracelet while Beverly waited.

When their attention came back to her Beverly pointed a finger at him, then at herself, and finally gestured widely to the jungle about the village, indicating as plainly as she could that she wanted him to take her for a walk. Firmly he shook his head, his companions muttering darkly.

Reluctantly Beverly removed the second bracelet. The procedure was the same as with the first: suspicion, consultation, and a refusal from the one she was trying to win to friendship. Perhaps she was mistaken but she thought the refusal was a little more reluctantly given this time.

She turned away and started back for her hut when someone touched her arm. It was the young warrior. He gestured at the third and remaining bracelet but Beverly shook her head. Then he pointed at her, the surrounding jungle and the last bracelet. He was willing to do as she wished for the third bracelet!

Beverly slipped the third and remaining bracelet from her wrist and held it out. She had to trust that he would keep his word. The native seized the bracelet and, after a wide, triumphant grin at his fellow warriors, walked to the edge of the clearing. There he paused and looked back, evidently expecting her to follow.

Without delay Beverly hurried after him, little realizing the consternation she caused among her friends who watched her go.

CHAPTER XIII

Alone

Beverly had counted on the natives' curiosity to see what she wanted in the jungle and, as long as she did not want to go alone, they must have decided to humor her.

The native walked beside her, taking his eyes from her only to admire the silver bracelets dangling at his belt. Evidently his new possessions meant added importance in the community because he walked with a spring in his step and his head high.

Beverly, having in mind that the missionary's village lay directly to the west, turned in that direction. Here she found opposition. The native leaped in front of her, gesticulating wildly, chattering in his native tongue. It was plain that he wanted her to go no farther in that direction. When Beverly persisted he put the point of his sword against her. He did not lower his sword and she started off again on a faint trail parallel to the village she had just left. He followed her in a friendly fashion as long as she made no attempt to leave the trail or turn away from the village. She dared not be too obvious in her intention, lest his suspicions be aroused and he summon his fellow warriors, but time was passing rapidly. The natives would be preparing for their coming sacrifice. She could not waste any more time. Somehow, she had to get rid of her guide.

But how? She sat down at the foot of a thick tree on a bed of moss to think over the situation. He squatted down in front of her, patient endurance on his copper face. Now that she was seated quietly she realized that the sound of drums from the village had grown in volume and tempo. Her guide noticed it, too, now and then casting a glance in the direction from which they had come. Plainly he wanted to return to his friends. At last he could endure it no longer. He leaped up and seized her wrist, but Beverly did not rise. She hung back, remaining seated at the foot of the tree. He poured a torrent of native lingo upon her but Beverly merely smiled and refused to move. Finally he sat down again, disgruntled and unhappy.

After awhile Beverly let her head fall forward and she feigned sleep. The native walked around the tree, stopped and listened attentively, then resumed his place opposite Beverly. When several moments had passed and she had not stirred, he got silently to his feet and faded into the bushes.

For several minutes Beverly remained perfectly still, afraid that he might be spying upon her from the depths of the thicket. But when there was no sound or movement she stood up and looked around. Apparently he had gone back to the village, intending to return before she wakened. How long he would leave her she did not know, but this was the opportunity she had been waiting for. She turned and plunged into the underbrush. From now on she was alone against the jungle.

At first her solitude did not mean much. She was buoyed up by the thought of rescuing her friends. But after hours of fighting through tangling vines, endeavoring to set some sort of course, and hearing strange noises in the brush, fear began to possess her. She visualized snakes in the low, clinging vines, alligators in the logs floating in dark jungle pools, and ferocious beasts in every whisper of a leaf.

"Beverly!" she said aloud. "Behave!"

Her voice came back to her, clear and true. She remembered the time she had been lost in the jungle in India. Panic had conquered her then. She would not let it do so again. She tried to make as much haste as possible, but the trail was faint and she was unfamiliar with jungle travel. She stumbled over gnarled roots; low-hanging branches scratched her face and hands. Once when she stopped to rest and leaned against a tree, what she thought was a thick vine moved and she knew it was a snake. She shuddered and moved away swiftly.

Without so much as a knife for protection, unarmed, afraid, could she possibly win through to her goal? She stood still and listened to the faint jungle sounds around her. Chattering monkeys, the dull beat of a distant tom-tom, a faint animal cry. It was shadowy and mysterious and she was totally alone.

The sun was rapidly sinking and Beverly knew that once darkness came she would be completely lost. Now she could guide herself by the faint rays of sunlight that seeped through the trees. However, when nothing but darkness lay around her she might as well give up, even though she still must be far from the small settlement she sought.

She wondered what was happening in the village she had left and if the native had returned to the spot where he had left her. The thought of Larry and the others spurred her on and she hastened her steps.

She circled a deep forest pool and suddenly burst out upon a small clearing. A scream was stifled on her lips and she closed her eyes, making a hasty effort to pull herself together.

Before her lay a skeleton, the bones white and dry against the green mossy ground. It was the skeleton of a man and the story of how he met his fate was all too clear, even to Beverly's inexperienced eyes. Arrows stuck from the surrounding trees and two of them even protruded from among the bones. A brown knapsack lay beside the fallen figure and the skeleton fingers reached mutely for a revolver lying a few feet away.

Beverly realized with a start that this unknown must be one of the men for whom Mike and Larry had been searching. Suppose her own search for Larry ended like this? She put the thought away from her and forced herself to reach for the dirty knapsack. It was almost empty but it did yield a small hunting knife and a flashlight whose beam of light was feeble. Her next move was to reluctantly pick up the revolver. She knew little about firearms, but she could determine that the gun still held two cartridges. She was afraid to fire it to see if it still worked, lest she should waste the two bullets. She might need them later.

With a final glance at the skeleton and a silent promise to bring Mike and Larry there so that the unknown need not lie forgotten forever, she went doggedly on her way. It was strange what new security she felt in the possession of the revolver, knife and flashlight. Just the touch of them lent her new courage.

She went on as swiftly as she could. It grew dark quickly, the shadows seeming more ominous and the night noises even more eerie than they had in the daytime. With the faint rays of the flashlight as illumination Beverly kept doggedly to what she hoped was a path. She tried to head directly west, into the spot where the sun had sunk from sight, stopping for only brief intervals of rest. She was exhausted and hungry but she dared not stop for long. It would be a waste of precious time during which anything could be happening to her friends.

Once she thought she would have to use the revolver she carried. There was a furious crashing in the underbrush. However, whatever had been there did not cross her path but went off into the jungle behind her. She had probably frightened him as much as he had her.

The moon was mounting in the heavens, its clear white light filtering through the trees. Beverly regarded it thankfully. It would be another night before it was full and, if Shirley was right, the natives probably would do nothing until the next night but work themselves into a frenzy.

Something hanging from a tree slapped against her and she emitted a scream of fear. Then she screamed again to let out some of the pent-up emotion within her. Her voice echoed back to her and then there was breathless silence as if all the jungle paused to listen.

"That," she thought wryly of her scream, "should clear the path ahead. I sound like a locomotive blowing off steam."

She laughed and felt better but her light mood was short-lived. Nervously glancing over her shoulder she thought she saw two green eyes staring at her. Once before she had been stalked and almost killed by a tiger. What was it someone had said—history repeats. Well, it couldn't be the same tiger for he had ended up as a rug. However, there were plenty of jaguars in the jungle. She moved a few feet and looked again. The green eyes were still staring at her. Maybe it was an owl. Did they have owls here? She fingered the cold steel of the revolver, hoping it was still in working condition.

It was strange. When she stopped to listen there was no sound—just the fixed stare of those eyes. When she moved on they did the same, keeping pace with her. It was like a cat playing with a mouse. What was he waiting for, Beverly wondered. If he meant to spring upon her, why didn't he do so and get it over with? Maybe he was working up an appetite first, she thought grimly. Should she turn her back on Mr. Green Eyes and let her imagination construe all sorts of horrible pictures of what could be happening behind her? Or should she suddenly whirl and shoot at him without considering his motives? On the other hand, perhaps she could lose him by sly maneuvers through the jungle growth. A shot might bring the natives out on her trail!

Once more she tried to hurry through the clinging, twisted jungle growth. Now, behind her, was not only her friends' plight and the natives to spur her on, but a silent thing that relentlessly dogged her footsteps.

She stumbled and fell more often now, exhausted and lost. Each time it was more of an effort to rise and go on. It was so tempting to lie still on the cool, wet moss in the darkness and forget about natives and snakes and green eyes.

The cry of a night bird startled her and she stumbled and fell once more. There was a movement behind her and she half rose, lifting the revolver. She pulled the trigger as a dark shape moved toward her. There was only a faint click as the gun did not go off.

Beverly did not realize that she screamed. She knew only that another dark shape had flung itself upon her, sheltering her from those terrible green eyes and a human voice spoke out of the blackness.

CHAPTER XIV

Rescue

"It is a dream," Beverly told herself after one glance around the room. It had to be a dream. It couldn't possibly be real.

She was in a small, clean room, sparsely furnished, and sunlight was streaming in the window. When her second glance took in the sight of her flashlight and revolver lying on a small wooden table beside a half-burnt candle, she knew it was no dream and sat up. She had been lying on a bed of dried grass covered by a worn brown blanket and she wondered how she had come to be there. Her watch showed nine o'clock. Hours had elapsed since her flight into the jungle. How long had she been sleeping and wasting precious time?

There was a stealthy movement at the door and she stifled a gasp. A jaguar stood there, eyes blinking sleepily at her. Round his neck he wore a wide leather collar.

"Do not be afraid," a kindly voice said from the window. "Geezo is friendly."

"Geezo," Beverly echoed faintly.

"I raised him from a kitten. How do you feel? I'm sorry I had to knock you down last night but Geezo was about to spring on you—playfully of course. I hope I didn't hurt you."

"It was a football tackle if I ever saw one," Beverly smiled. "You must be the medical missionary."

"The people call me Father Dennis," he smiled.

"I was looking for you," Beverly continued hastily. "We haven't a second to lose. You've got to help me!"

Her host left the window and entered the room through the little doorway. Now that she had a better look at him she was surprised at his youth. Despite the black beard and long, brown friar's cloak there was the agility of youth in his movements. He seated himself on a low stool and smiled at her.

"I will be happy to help you in any way I can. Suppose you tell me your story."

Beverly had pictured herself dramatically bursting in upon an old missionary surrounded by his converts. Instead she was reciting the story of her and her friends' plight calmly, as if it were only an interesting story. This man had that effect upon her. He calmed her and seemed to take away her troubles. It was as if by merely pouring out her story to him everything would be all right.

When Beverly finished her story the man smiled kindly and stood up.

"Come with me, please. I have something to show you."

Wondering, Beverly followed the missionary from the small house, the jungle animal stalking silently behind them, to another, even smaller bamboo house.

"I will start at once to make preparations that we may go and help your friends," Father Dennis said. "If you will wait here for me I shall return in a little while. Please go inside."

More mystified, Beverly watched him walk away, a smile on his face. Then she turned and lifted the skin that hung across the doorway. Stepping into the darkened interior she paused until her eyes grew accustomed to the change from bright sunlight. Gradually she made out objects, a table and a chair, a bowl of fruit and a jug of water. As she moved farther into the room she became aware of a figure lying on a rough bunk at the back of the room, a white, ragged figure that did not move. Remembering the missionary's smile she went closer, her heart racing.

The gaunt figure was scarcely recognizable as the buoyant, smiling Larry that had left her in New York. His eyes were closed but he was breathing regularly. His face was thin and terribly white and there was a red, ugly gash across his forehead. Hot tears stung Beverly's eyes. This really was the end of the trail. She had found him at last.

Beverly's first impulse was to fly to Father Dennis for help, then she reasoned that the missionary had brought her here. He knew about Larry and had guessed from her story that he was the one she was searching for. The missionary must be sure, too, that Larry was all right or he wouldn't have left him. Yet she felt frightened. How ill he must have been!

She put her hand lightly on his forehead. It was hot to her touch. She took her handkerchief and wet it from the jug on the table. She bathed his forehead and he stirred.

"Thanks." His voice was a mere whisper. "Did you go for my friend?"

"Don't try to talk," Beverly cautioned softly.

His eyes opened and he struggled up on one elbow.

"Beverly! Is it really you?"

"Yes," she smiled. "Now lie still. You mustn't get excited."

"Excited," he groaned, dropping back. "A miracle happens and you tell me not to get excited! Beverly, how did you get here? How long has it been——"

She sat on the edge of his bunk and he held her hands tightly while she told him her story. Father Dennis came in just as she finished.

"Everything is arranged."

Beverly rose. She was torn between the desire to stay with Larry and to guide the missionary to her friends.

"Where are you going?" Larry demanded.

"To get the others," Beverly replied.

"We will be back soon," the missionary added. "Do not be afraid. Try to rest."

"Rest! I'm going with you," Larry declared.

"You can't," Beverly said, alarmed. "You aren't well enough."

"It was only exhaustion and hunger and maybe a touch of fever," Larry smiled. He stood up, swaying slightly. "Say I can go, Father Dennis?"

"Emergency lends great strength sometimes," the missionary said, watching the younger man closely. "We will have chairs for you and Miss Gray."

"Can we go at once?" Beverly asked. "Anything might be happening."

"Do not distress yourself," Father Dennis said kindly. "We shall leave at once. With Charlie to guide us we shall make good time and be at the village before the moon is at its height tonight."

The missionary went out and Beverly heard his voice raised in a command to the natives. A second later a huge native, so tall he had to stoop to enter the little house, came to them and announced:

"Me Charlie. You come."

Beverly and Larry followed him outside. The villagers were gathered about a huge ceremonial drum and in the center of the circle stood the missionary. He came forward to them while Beverly viewed the natives with some misgivings. They looked almost as ferocious as the ones from whom she had just fled.

"They are friendly enough," Father Dennis assured her. "They are as gentle and curious as children. You mustn't mind them staring at you. You would stare at one of them, too, if he suddenly appeared on Times Square."

Beverly smiled and tried to appear perfectly at ease, but all the while she was screaming inwardly for haste and action.

There were no extensive plans to be made. The natives merely snatched up their spears and were ready to go. Two natives carried a roughly fashioned cane chair secured to sturdy poles which rested on the men's shoulders. Beverly was assisted into this; Larry into a similar one behind her. The party set off with the missionary in the lead and beside him walked Geezo. It was another of the unbelievable sights of the jungle, the tall, kindly man striding on, nobleness of purpose in every step, and beside him, treading the stealthy step of his kind, the fierce, treacherous jungle cat.

"I can't believe it," Beverly murmured. "Aren't you ever afraid of him, Father Dennis?"

"No, my child. Geezo and I understand each other."

"But animals are treacherous," persisted Beverly. "Especially here in the jungle. Aren't you ever afraid he will revert to his primitive instincts and attack you?"

"Sometime he may," was the slow, untroubled answer, "but I do not think of it. He looks upon me as his master and his friend and as long as I deal with him in kindness I do not fear him. It is only when he senses fear that he is aroused. You noticed when you were first afraid of him he snarled at you. Then he was dangerous. Now you do not seem to fear him and he pays no attention to you."

"That doesn't mean I trust him," Beverly laughed, regarding the animal warily, as if he might understand her words. "I intend to keep you between us, if you don't mind."

They went swiftly, the missionary faultlessly choosing the right paths, Beverly and Larry swaying in their chairs, smiling at each other over the heads of the natives. At the pace they went the way was not nearly as long as it had been for Beverly when she sought the missionary. At the end of two hours they came into sight of their quarry and the party halted.

"You will wait here," the missionary said. "I will try

to speak with them in peace." He went on toward the village, Geezo striding silently behind him.

It was preposterous, one man and a jaguar against a horde of savages. Beverly and Larry watched breathlessly as the kindly man and his strange pet walked into the center of the dancers gathered about a fire. At his appearance there was an instant of stunned, surprised silence. Then the witch doctor came forward, looking even more evil than Beverly had remembered. He spoke in his guttural language and the missionary replied in kind. Beverly could see the amazement of the other natives that this man should speak to them in their own tongue!

Beside her the bulk of Charlie bristled to attention. She wished frantically that she could understand what was being said. As it was, she had to rely on her eyes to note the emotions on the faces of the natives and on her intuition to tell her all was not going well.

Neither the witch doctor nor the chief of the tribe was to be influenced by the missionary's peace talk. Their tribal ceremonies had reached their height and they were not to be restrained. Angry mutterings came from the witch doctor's followers and they stirred rebelliously, closing in a tight circle about the missionary, almost obstructing him from view. The witch doctor let out a shrill shout and raised his stick in the air. When the blow fell the natives danced in glee and the man who had walked in unafraid and smiling lay on the ground, Geezo standing over him snarling defiance.

Charlie let out a growl, brandishing his spear in a signal to his fellow tribesmen. It was to be a battle and there was no hope of averting it. Larry pulled her to one side as the missionary's followers charged with a great deal of noise and were met with a hail of flying spears and arrows.

For a precious, wasted moment Beverly and Larry watched the fray and then fought their way to the nearest hut. It was the one in which Shirley and Lenora were imprisoned. A bitter struggle was going on and the guards had deserted their posts to join in the fight. Beverly freed the girls while Larry went to rescue Jim, Roger and David. Then, while the young men fought their way to the missionary, Beverly started toward Mike's hut. She was halfway there when a great rumble as of thunder shook the earth beneath her feet. She was flung to the ground while behind her she heard Lenora scream "Earthquake!"

Beverly struggled up from where the first shock had flung her. The world about them was in chaos. Natives cowered on the ground. Larry and Jim were helping the missionary to rise. Again Beverly started toward Mike's hut. She had just reached the entrance when another rumble began and the ground rocked crazily beneath her feet. She fell forward as Larry called her name. The hut crumbled.

The natives were on their knees in an agony of fright and lay writhing as the earth rose and fell. Cracks appeared in the earth's surface. Cries came from the jungle as animals stampeded in terror. The frail native houses collapsed as if made of matchsticks. Then suddenly there was silence. Not a breath of wind stirred the trees. For a moment there was no movement or sound of any kind.

"Beverly!" Lenora screamed.

"I saw her going toward Mike's hut," Shirley gasped. "Over there——"

"In what was a hut," Lenora put in fearfully. "It's a jumbled mass now."

"Come on," Jim said and started across the clearing after Larry.

While the young men worked feverishly extricating first Mike and then Beverly, the girls administered first aid to the injured. Father Dennis was their first patient. The missionary was not seriously hurt and soon took charge of things, patiently and kindly directing the now subdued natives, and treating Mike and Beverly.

"I'm scared," Lenora whispered to Shirley, seeing Beverly's white face.

"We don't have time to be scared," Shirley returned, and went to the aid of Father Dennis.

It was a tense little group that hovered over the slender doctor as he strove to do his best, hampered as he was by lack of medical aids.

"Do something!" Larry urged. "You've got to do something."

"Everything will be done that can be done," the missionary assured them. "Both the young man and Miss Gray will be all right."

"Are you sure?" Larry insisted.

"Of course he's sure," Beverly herself said, sitting up with a groan. "What hit me?"

"Darling, you were kissed by a whole house," Lenora said. "You've even got splinters in your hair."

"Is Larry——"

"Here," that young man said, dropping to one knee beside her.

"Is the earthquake over?" Beverly asked.

"I hope——" Shirley began. "No! Here it comes again!"

Lenora flung herself flat on the ground, her fingers in her ears, while the others clung to each other and tried stubbornly to stay on their feet as the earth shook and rumbled beneath them.

CHAPTER XV

Homeward Bound

"HERE, pussy, pussy," Lenora leaned out the window and called vainly to Geezo who paced back and forth before the hut, his head disdainfully averted.

"That is no way to call a wildcat," Shirley laughed.

It was two days after the earthquake, and here, in the quiet village where the missionary lived, the people were busily engaged in reconstructing the buildings that had been wrecked. Since their escape from the head-hunters, the girls had occupied the missionary's house, which had been one of the least damaged and the first to be repaired. Early that morning the young men had gone out to seek the skeleton Beverly had found on her flight to the missonary. In the girls' enforced idleness time was beginning to hang heavily on their hands.

"Shouldn't they be back by now?" Shirley asked. "We are supposed to leave at noon."

"I hate to leave without the emerald," Lenora said.

"That emerald!" Shirley exclaimed. "It was the cause of all our trouble. I never want to see it again."

"But it is such a waste—leaving it there," Lenora persisted. "I wonder if David would go with me to get it?"

"Why don't you leave it alone?" Shirley demanded "Everything is all right now. Why stir up more trouble?"

"You are just superstitious," Lenora said with a toss of her head. "I think I'll go over and cheer Mike."

Beverly and Shirley watched her leave their hut, drop a careless hand on Geezo's head and the two of them stroll across the clearing.

"The next thing you know she will want to take Geezo home with her," Shirley said. "Wouldn't he look cute sitting in the middle of our apartment!"

Beverly laughed. "The past two days have been too quiet for Lenora."

"We've had enough excitement for my taste," Shirley

declared. "Jungles—head-hunters—earthquakes—oh, for the peace and quiet of Forty-second Street!"

"It won't be long now," Beverly comforted her. "In two days we will be on the *Susabella* and homeward bound."

"Never more to roam!" Shirley vowed solemnly. "I am going to settle down to work in *Lonesome Lady*. How about you? Are you going back to Hollywood?"

Beverly shook her head. "I don't think so. There are too many things I want to do in New York."

"Here they come," Shirley announced at the window. "Larry looks worn out."

"He shouldn't have gone," Beverly said. "Father Dennis warned him that it would tax his strength."

The girls went out to meet the young men returning with spades over their shoulders, overheated and exhausted.

"We found the second man about a hundred yards away from the first," Roger told them quietly.

"We buried them near a quiet pool," added David. "Poor fellows. All because they wanted that emerald."

"Lenora wants it now," Shirley said with a glance at the blonde girl.

"Forget it," Jim advised. "We went back to look things over. The head-hunters have deserted their village and the earthquake left the city where the emerald was a mass of jumbled rock. It is gone and we will never know whether it is at the bottom of all the rock or whether the head-hunters succeeded in taking it with them."

"That's good," Shirley said with satisfaction. "Now we can start for home."

The next day they said good-bye to the missionary and started off once more.

Travel through the jungle was slow and difficult work for Mike with his injured ankle, but with the aid of a crutch carved from a tree limb by his friends he managed fairly well to keep up with their pace.

By nightfall they had come to the river. And there, waiting for them, as the missionary had promised there would be, were boats and native paddlers to transport them back to the *Susabella.*

They did not camp that night but dozed fitfully in the boats, eager to reach civilization as soon as possible. The next afternoon, tired and hot, they came into sight of the white, gleaming yacht.

As they drew nearer they were amazed at the activity

along the riverbank. Inquiries soon revealed that the earthquake had been felt even here and much of the town was a shambles. Mike was made comfortable aboard the *Susabella,* then Jim, Larry, and Beverly volunteered to get a doctor. It proved more difficult than they had anticipated, since most of the doctors were busy with victims of the earthquake. Buildings which once had been stores or homes were now mere piles of debris. In some cases whole streets were closed to traffic.

"How quickly things happen," Beverly murmured. "When we were here before this was a busy city."

"In a way, the earthquake was a blessing," Jim said. "The authorities have been trying to clean up the city by getting rid of a lot of those old, rickety buildings but the people refused to accept modern ideas. Now there will have to be new houses erected and their living conditions will be greatly improved."

"There's some good in everything if we look for it," Larry murmured. "Do you like it here, Jim?"

"I did," Jim said frankly, "but now I want to go home. I want to see the New York skyline and snow in Central Park. I want some of my mother's home-made apple pie and a thick steak smothered with mushrooms. I want to ride the subway and mix with the crowd in Times Square. I want——"

"Why don't you come home with us?" Beverly asked.

"All I needed was the invitation," Jim grinned. "I'll go on the *Susabella* if you can stop off at my friend's plantation while I pick up my things."

"Roger will arrange that," Larry assured him, "and we'll all go home together."

They found a Spanish doctor who accompanied them to the yacht and gave Mike the attention and care Father Dennis had not been able to give.

That night, as they were dressing for their first dinner on shipboard, the boat began its journey down the river to the sea.

"Sailing, sailing," Lenora sang as she struggled into her dress. "Here, one of you, zip me, please."

Beverly came to her friend's aid and manipulated the zipper.

"You look very fetching in that green dress," Lenora continued, inspecting her friend. "Bows in your hair and stars in your eyes."

"My, aren't you perky," Shirley commented with a smile.

"Of course I am," Lenora said. "We are going home."

"Not losing your taste for adventure, are you?" Shirley asked.

"Everything turned out all right," added Beverly. "Are you ready?"

"I'll race you up on deck," Lenora proposed. "The last one up has to sing for her supper."

"I refuse to race," Shirley said lazily. "Lenora, fasten my bracelet for me, will you?"

Beverly left the cabin and Lenora grinned at Shirley.

"I get it. The tactful thing is to let her meet Larry alone."

"Well, after what they've been through——" Shirley smiled. "She hasn't really been alone with him at all."

"Now it is Larry, Beverly, and Jim," Lenora murmured. "The Three Musketeers. I think I'll go and annoy Mike. He's a stubborn Irishman but I like him."

"As much as Terry?" Shirley inquired.

Lenora paused to glance out the porthole, her back to Shirley.

"Terry is three thousand miles away," she said in a subdued voice.

"That's a long way," Shirley murmured.

When Lenora turned around Shirley was amazed to see tears in her eyes.

"I'm sorry, Lenora. I shouldn't have brought that up," Shirley said hastily.

"I was a goon," Lenora shrugged. "I'm not usually the weepy kind. Let's forget it. I'll see you at dinner."

Shirley went up on deck. Beverly was there, sitting between Larry and Jim. Shirley thought of what Lenora had said. She remembered how often she had seen Beverly between Larry and Jim and wondered what the latter's return to New York might mean in Beverly's life.

Life on board the ship was a lazy one, and after the uncertainty and fears of the past weeks it was good to relax after a delicious dinner, to dance on deck, play bridge, or merely sit and gaze at the stars overhead.

In such a mood of placid contentment they dropped anchor in a little harbor and traveled overland two miles to the plantation owned by Jim's friend, Colonel Scott, a retired army officer. The plantation house was a low, rambling affair, cool and inviting. The colonel was hospitality personified. He insisted that they stay a few days and the young people were delighted with the invitation.

They played tennis on the court in back of the house, rode about the plantation with their host, or merely sat in the low comfortable chairs on the veranda and chatted.

At last Jim's things were packed aboard the *Susabella,* good-byes were said, and the yacht again got underway.

"It is a shame," Lenora declared, hanging over the rail. "We are in South America and yet we haven't seen much of it. I want to go ashore somewhere and see some sights."

"Let's," Shirley agreed.

Roger looked at Jim. "You are the guide down here, Jim. Do you know a spot where Lenora can satisfy her suppressed desire for a rumba?"

"I know just the place," Jim nodded. "It is a little town on the coast. We could put in there tomorrow night if you like."

Everyone else liked the idea and at sunset the next day they dropped anchor in a tiny crowded harbor and prepared to see the town.

"I," Lenora announced, "am going to find me a handsome señor and learn to rumba."

"I am more than a year ahead of you," Jim laughed. "I'll give you lessons. We'll go to Mamma Theo's. She has the best rumba music in all South America."

"But first we are going to see the city," Shirley said.

And they did. They had to leave Mike on the boat but they lavishly promised to bring him half the city as a souvenir. They fared forth in gay hilarity, exclaiming over the shops, the abundance of flowers and fruit, and the smiling friendliness of the people.

On one occasion when they crossed a street Larry stood still to gaze back the way they had come.

"What's the matter?"

"That man—I thought I recognized him," Larry murmured. "It can't be—yet I'm sure. Wait for me. I'll be back in a minute." He dodged through traffic and disappeared into a building across the street.

The others gazed interestedly at the shop windows, walking slowly, and in a very short time Larry was back with them.

"It wasn't the man I thought it was after all," he announced, and the matter was forgotten.

They dined and danced and walked until they were exhausted, coming back to the *Susabella* just as the sky was beginning to grow light with dawn.

They said good nights on deck and stumbled sleepily down to their respective cabins. They were to sail that afternoon and despite the hour at which they had retired they were on deck about noon.

"Well, let's sail," Lenora suggested, hanging over the rail watching the harbor. "What are we waiting for?"

"Larry," Beverly answered.

"Where is he? Still in bed?"

"He went ashore," Beverly explained.

"If he doesn't come soon, we won't be able to sail until tomorrow," Roger declared.

"Why not?" Lenora wanted to know.

"There are such things as tides, my pet," Shirley laughed. "You can't sail a boat if you haven't any water."

"I forgot about that," Lenora giggled.

"Where did he go, Bev?" David asked.

"I don't know," Beverly returned. "All he said was that he had an errand to do and he would be back before sailing time."

"Maybe he meant sailing time tomorrow," Lenora offered.

"He'll be here," Roger said confidently.

"Unless he ran into another earthquake," Shirley smiled.

"Speaking of earthquakes," David grinned, "Jim and

Lenora made the buildings totter a bit last night with their rumba."

"That was nothing," Lenora said modestly. "Wait until I've practiced a bit."

"Here comes Larry," Shirley interrupted.

Larry, out of breath, his face red, necktie flying, one pocket of his coat torn, was running toward the yacht. Close behind him raced a tall figure in a white sailor suit, blonde hair rumpled and a cut on one cheek to which he pressed a bloodstained handkerchief.

"Where have you been?" David demanded as Larry bounded up the gangplank.

"Is that a shiner you have?" Roger seconded.

"Larry! Do you have a black eye?" Lenora asked interestedly.

"This is Lieutenant Cary, U.S.N.," Larry introduced breathlessly. "He is sailing with us."

The others acknowledged the introduction with silent nods, too surprised to say a word.

"Anchors aweigh, Roger!" Larry cried. "Let's get going."

"Seems to me you are in a hurry to leave," Lenora offered.

"Who is chasing you?" added Beverly.

"Now you are teasing me," Larry grinned. "Let's go, Roger."

"Okay. If you'll come with me, Lieutenant Cary, I'll give orders to sail and then we'll treat that cut you have."

The navy man followed Roger and a buzz of talk immediately sprang up.

"Who is he?"

"Where did you meet him?"

"What happened to you?"

"We got caught in a crowd," Larry laughed. "That's all."

"That's not all and we know it," Lenora declared. "However, if that is all you are going to tell us——" she walked off to go below deck. The others followed to find Roger and the new arrival.

The gangplank was pulled aboard and the *Susabella* glided away from the pier. As the water widened between the ship and the shore Larry leaned upon the rail, a wide grin on his face.

"It must have been good," Beverly said at his side.

"It was the best fight I ever——" he stopped. "You caught me that time."

"What was it?" Beverly asked.

"A free-for-all," Larry said. "Somebody didn't like the lieutenant. Another fellow didn't like me."

"You make it all sound very mysterious," Beverly declared.

"Don't bother your head about it," Larry smiled.

"But I scent a story for Charlie Blaine," Beverly returned.

"There's no story. At least not one that can be printed," he assured her. "The world is aflame with war and hatred and bitterness, Beverly. Maybe what we did today will help to keep it a little farther away from us."

Beverly knew he had told her all he was going to about the affair, but she realized it must have been important.

On shore a cloud of smoke was growing over a group of buildings. There was a sound behind them and the navy man came to lean on the rail beside Larry. The two men looked at the smoke, then at each other, and grinned happily. It was plain to Beverly that they knew what the fire was and how it had started, but she knew, too, that they would never tell the story.

CHAPTER XVI

The Susabella

THE bow of the *Susabella* cut through the water, dividing the green waves into white-capped columns of glistening waves. The sun made sparkling diamonds of the spray.

"There is something about standing at a boat rail that affects me," Lenora said dreamily. "It must be a hand-me-down from a pirate ancestor."

"It is the lure of far places and strange lands," Beverly added. "Almost like homesickness even though you've never seen them."

"I should have been a sailor," Lenora continued. "I love the briny deep." She looked around her, carefully noting the positions of her friends. Since there was no one within hearing distance she turned back to Beverly.

"Bev, do you think there is anything strange about Lieutenant Cary?"

"Strange?" Beverly murmured.

"I mean," Lenora continued in a low voice, "the way he came on board and—well, just everything about him." She leaned closer. "Do you think he could be a spy?"

Beverly laughed. "Of course not. Larry told us that the lieutenant's ship sailed without him and since he has to get back to New York, why shouldn't he sail with us?"

"Why, indeed," Lenora said. "What about the fight he and Larry were in? Didn't that make you suspicious?"

Shirley came on deck at that point and walked over to them.

Beverly was glad when the two girls went off to play shuffleboard. Lenora's questions about the lieutenant were unanswerable. Beverly, too, wondered about the man, but there was nothing definite on which to base her suspicions. Larry, and now David, too, spent a great deal of time with him. They were an effective blockade against the others' questions and curiosity. It was almost as if they were protecting him from the other young people on the yacht. Beverly knew her friends had noticed this, but they apparently had accepted the situation. Only she, and now Lenora, seemed to be suspicious of their motives.

Beverly lingered alone in the bow of the boat to watch the sunset. Presently Larry came up and sat in the chair next to hers.

"This is the life!" he exclaimed.

"I could sail on and on forever," she agreed.

"What?" he teased. "No *Tribune?* No typewriter?"

"Why don't you tell me what is going on?" she smiled.

"Beverly, the reporter!" he laughed.

"Tell me about it," she commanded.

"I might as well," he smiled. "Lieutenant Cary is on a mission from the State Department."

"Then he isn't really a sailor?"

"It is as good a disguise as any," Larry returned. "He has been in South America several weeks and during that time he has accumulated positive proof that there are foreign powers at work stirring up the people, turning them against the United States. Do you remember when we were walking about the town that night I thought I saw a man I knew?"

Beverly nodded.

"Well, it was one of the men I used to work with in the Secret Service. He asked me to help get the lieutenant out of town and safely back to the United States. I agreed to meet him early the next morning and bring the lieutenant to the yacht. When we went for Lieutenant Cary we found him unconscious, his room ransacked, and all his papers gone. He knew the men who had done it. He had seen them following him, so we went after them. We got his papers back after a fight, and while the lieutenant and I came to the *Susabella,* the other man set fire to the headquarters of the gang. I don't think they'll do any more plotting there."

"That is why you were grinning in such a self-satisfied manner when you saw the smoke from the fire on shore," Beverly said.

Larry stood up and drew her to her feet. "It is all over now and so far we are safe. Let's get dressed for dinner or all the others will be ahead of us."

"We were beginning to think you might have fallen overboard," Lenora declared as Beverly entered the girls' cabin. "Behold!" She had fastened a paper flower in her hair and was viewing herself in the mirror. "Aren't I elegant?"

"Something the cat forgot," Shirley giggled and dodged as Lenora hurled a powder puff at her.

"I think it is simply dee-vine," Lenora declared. "You know, I think after dinner I shall develop some of the pictures I took on our trip. Would you like to work in the darkroom with me, Shirley my pet?"

"Why don't you ask Mike?" Shirley returned teasingly. "I'm sure he'd love to help you."

This time Lenora did not miss when she threw a pillow. The girls' merriment continued all through dinner. It was contagious and soon everyone joined in the hilarity. Even Lieutenant Cary seemed to be enjoying himself.

After dinner Lenora and Mike and Shirley and Roger went into Woo Fong's kitchen to develop some of the snapshots Lenora had taken and the other young people took the radio on deck. Jim and David chatted with Lieutenant Cary while Beverly and Larry danced. Chinese lanterns strung along the deck shed a faint, mellow glow. The waves splashed against the boat as the bow cut cleanly through the water. Into the peaceful scene burst Lenora.

"Stop the boat! Stop the boat! We have just gotten the most brilliant idea."

"We?" Larry laughed.

"What is it?" Beverly asked.

Lenora took a deep breath and beamed upon them.

"I have some more film to finish and I have to buy developer. In addition to that, Woo Fong says he has run out of pineapple juice. Besides," she finished with a grin, "we want to see Havana."

"We want to see Havana," murmured Jim.

"Yes, we do," Lenora said. "Don't we, Beverly?"

"Oh, yes!" Beverly agreed, catching Lenora's wink and playing up. "We want to buy perfume——"

"And coconuts," finished Lenora. "Roger thinks it is a good idea, don't you, Roger?" She appealed to the young man just stepping on deck.

"What can I do?" Roger appealed to Jim and Larry.

"I suppose we shall see Havana," David laughed over his brother's shoulder. "Ah, the appeal of the tropics!"

Just as the first streaks of dawn were lighting the sky the *Susabella* came into the quiet waters of Havana Harbor, passed the Morro Castle, and slid into berth beside a huge ocean liner. The young people stood on deck in the damp, gray early morning and watched the fishing boats glide past.

"Where's the glamour?" Lenora demanded. "I want to see the gay, exciting Havana the travel folders tell about."

"Can you be glamorous at seven in the morning?" Shirley returned.

Lenora giggled. "I am usually asleep at that hour."

"Here they come," Roger said, peering over the side.

"Who is coming?" Shirley asked.

"The boys who dive for coins," David explained. He reached into his pocket and tossed a coin over the side. It flashed in the air and disappeared beneath the surface of the water. Brown, eager, determined swimmers streaked for the spot where the coin had disappeared. One boy emerged triumphant, holding the coin aloft as proof that he had retrieved it. Then he slipped it into his mouth and joined his companions in noisy begging for more coins.

Their first picture of the city was one of old buildings and narrow streets crowded with people, until their taxi driver and self-appointed guide took them into the newer sections of town and showed them the sights of which the natives were most proud.

The girls declared their intention of going shopping as soon as the stores opened and since the young men were not interested in that, they proposed to separate for a few hours and meet at the yacht for lunch.

The girls invaded the shops and bought perfume, post cards, necklaces, and everything that appealed to them, and then proceeded to wrangle with a street merchant over the price of his enormous straw hats. They returned from their shopping tour laden with packages. Under Lenora's and Shirley's guidance the taxi driver carried their parcels aboard the *Susabella.* Beverly was about to follow when her attention was attracted by a group of two men huddled together in the shadows of the pier. One was Lieutenant Cary, and again Beverly felt that stirring of curiosity about him.

When he saw her watching him, he left his companions and walked over to her.

"I'm taking a plane from here, Miss Gray, so I'll say good-bye. It has been a pleasure to know you. Perhaps we will meet again some day. Bon voyage!" He stood back and saluted her in true Navy fashion.

"Happy landing!" she returned and watched him stride off with his two friends. Suddenly she became aware that a man had detached himself from the shadows of a building and was following the lieutenant and his companions. At the corner Lieutenant Cary waved good-bye to the men who had been with him and walked off alone. Beverly turned away and then looked back. The lone watcher was slowly trailing after the lieutenant.

A warning note sounded within her. All that Larry had told her came rushing back. If Lieutenant Cary's enemies had tried once to silence him, of course they would try again! And the lieutenant thought he was safe. He would not be prepared for their next attack.

Instantly Beverly began running. If she cut through the street she was on, perhaps she could head off the lieutenant and warn him. But the street opened onto a narrow alley and that one onto another. She was lost in the maze of unfamiliar lanes and it took precious moments to retrace her steps.

When she got back to her starting point there was no one in sight. She hurried along the way the lieutenant had gone. She ran two blocks before she spied her quarry far ahead of her, then saw the lieutenant signal a taxi. The man who was following him did the same. Frantically Beverly looked around for a third taxi. She found a wheezy old car with a grinning driver and told him to follow the other two cars. He obliged with no great burst of speed and twice she had to tell him to hurry lest she lose sight of the cars ahead. It was impossible to think of passing the second car to reach the lieutenant. Her taxi couldn't do it. The best she could hope for was to keep them in sight and reach the lieutenant when he stopped.

They left the narrow streets of the old city behind them and drove out wide, palm-bordered avenues into the country. Now and then they passed through tiny hamlets of small one-room houses. Children and dogs roamed the streets and stared curiously at the car.

Beverly wondered what Shirley and Lenora were thinking of her disappearance. Her next thought was: "How am I going to pay for the taxi?" She had spent her money on the shopping tour and had not stopped to think of that when she engaged the taxi. However, if she succeeded in reaching Lieutenant Cary, she felt sure that he would lend her enough for taxi fare.

Off to the left, behind a deserted farm, loomed several large buildings. Hangars for airplanes! The lieutenant's taxi drew to a halt. He jumped out, paid the driver and hastened into one of the buildings. The second car pulled up and its occupant rushed over to where an airplane was warming up.

Beverly leaped out of her car the moment it slid to a halt and ran into the building which the lieutenant had entered. He was talking to a man behind a huge desk and looked around as the door slammed behind her.

"Miss Gray! What are you doing here?"

Beverly motioned out the window. "Evidently the people who tried to murder you in South America are going to try again. That man followed you from the dock. I thought I should warn you."

"And now he is talking to the pilot of my plane!" Lieutenant Cary exclaimed. "I am indebted to you, Miss Gray. How they found me I don't know, but obviously I can't get into that plane. If I did——" he looked around. "I've got to get out of here."

"I'm coming with you," Beverly said at once.

He led the way out a back door. A motorcycle was standing there and the lieutenant climbed onto the driver's seat, motioning Beverly into the sidecar. They were off in a burst of noise and a cloud of dust, heading back to town through small, muddy side roads. It was a wild ride. Beverly had all she could do to hang on as the car swayed and threatened to topple over as they skidded around corners. She looked back once and saw a taxi speeding after them. The lieutenant had seen it, too, for the motorcycle leaped forward in a fresh burst of speed.

"Don't worry, we'll lose him," Lieutenant Cary shouted to her.

Beverly felt like reminding him that, though they wanted to lose the spy, they also wanted to remain in one piece. Corners were rounded with the machine tilted at a perilous angle. Ruts in the road were taken without slackening speed. Time and again they narrowly missed running down unsuspecting pedestrians or wrapping themselves around a tree. As they roared on, shattering the peace of country lanes, chickens fled squawking from their path and farmers stopped their work to stare in amazement.

At last they drove off the road into the shadowed yard of a small farm. The house was unpainted and weather-beaten. Beyond the building were small chicken houses and rows upon rows of pineapple plants.

"We'll stay here until we are sure there is no one following us," the lieutenant said. "What's the matter?"

"I never had such a wild ride in my life," Beverly laughed as she climbed out of the car. "Where are we?"

"This is a farm of a friend of mine. Oh, there he is!"

A man came toward them.

"Hello, Juan."

"Señor!"

"We would like to rest here for a while, Juan," the lieutenant said. "Can you put the motorcycle some place where it won't be seen from the road?"

"Certainly, Señor. Please come."

They followed Juan around the house. He put the motorcycle into a shed and they sat in the cool shade while a slender young girl brought them tall glasses of pineapple juice. They had been sitting there about five minutes when there was the sound of an automobile in the front yard. Instantly they were on the alert. Juan went around to see what was happening while Beverly and the lieutenant waited. He was back in a moment, a puzzled frown on his face.

"I do not understand, Señor."

"What is it, Juan?"

"The man only wishes his money, Señor."

"My taxi driver!" Beverly exclaimed. "I forgot him!"

Lieutenant Cary laughed and gave Juan the money to pay the man. Then he went to get the motorcycle.

"Are we leaving so soon?" Beverly asked.

"If your taxi driver could follow us anyone else might, too," was the reply.

Reluctantly Beverly climbed into the car again, and they were off with a spluttering roar. She tried to think of the story this would make. A man with important government papers being pursued across Cuba!

"You probably could get away quicker by yourself," she shouted above the roar of the motor.

"By this time they know you are with me," he shouted back. "It would not be safe to let you out of my sight."

She hadn't thought of that. Now the chase became a personal danger.

CHAPTER XVII

A Mission

THE motorcycle skidded to a stop before a telegraph office and the lieutenant hopped off.

"Got to send a wire. Won't be a moment."

While he was inside the small office Beverly noticed a black, shiny limousine draw up on the opposite side of the street. She was aware of a woman sitting in it watching her. The woman leaned forward a moment to look out the window, then drew back into the shadows. Beverly caught a clear glimpse of her face, however, and was left with a haunting impression of having seen her before. But where?

Lieutenant Cary hurried across the pavement and climbed onto his machine again. Beverly glanced uneasily over her shoulder at the black automobile. It had gone half a block and was now turning around to head in the same direction they were going.

"Did you notice the woman in that car?" Beverly asked the lieutenant. "I have a feeling I've seen her before, but I don't remember where or under what circumstances."

"I didn't get a close look at her," the lieutenant replied, starting the motorcycle.

"Her car is following us," Beverly remarked quietly.

He grinned. "Here we go again!"

The motorcycle abruptly turned a corner and plunged down a dark, narrow street, to turn again and again until Beverly felt hopelessly lost.

"That ought to do it," Lieutenant Cary declared, relaxing. "We don't want to get too far away. I want to see you safely on that boat with your friends."

"How will you get home?" Beverly asked. "You can't ride the motorcycle all the way to Washington."

He laughed. "I wouldn't want to ride that far on this thing. No, I shall take a plane—if I'm able to rent one."

"Where do you carry your papers?" Beverly asked curiously. "I always thought diplomats and such carried bulky brief cases."

"I've sent most of my reports home but the most important one is here." He tapped the breast pocket of his coat. "It's a good thing I'm not trying to hide a box of jewels or a roll of tapestry with all the dodging I've had to do."

"Tapestry! The Countess!" Beverly exclaimed. "That's who it was! Oh, my goodness!"

"What who was?" he asked.

Beverly glanced over her shoulder. "Several months ago my friends and I had an experience with some international spies. One or two were sent to prison but the Countess, who was really only a thief, escaped. I'm sure that was she in the black sedan."

"She was connected with the Ghost Ring, wasn't she?" the lieutenant asked. "Larry told me something about it. So you are the girl who helped on that case." He looked at her with new respect. "I picked a good partner for this chase."

"The Countess must have come to Cuba when she fled from New York," Beverly continued thoughtfully. "But how did she find us and why is she following us?"

"You said yourself that she is a thief," Lieutenant Cary smiled. "In troubled times like these the clever thief can make a good deal of money spying, selling information——"

"I thought only men did dangerous things like that——" Beverly began.

"It doesn't matter if it is a man or woman, if he or she is ruthless enough."

"We should let my friends know we are all right," Beverly murmured after a moment. "They will be wondering what happened."

"I'll call the hotel and have someone deliver a message," Lieutenant Cary agreed. "They planned on having dinner there, I know. We must have some dinner, too."

"I was wondering when you would get around to that," Beverly laughed.

"We'll go to the Havana Gardens," he proposed. "We can eat at a little table outdoors in the garden. The food is good and the place is not too crowded. The owner is a friend of mine."

"You seem to have friends just at the right spots," Beverly remarked.

"I lived in Cuba for many years," he explained.

They turned off the road through a wooden archway and approached a one-story, dark, wooden building. Lieutenant Cary parked the motorcycle before the door where several other cars were standing, and they walked around to the back of the house where small tables with red-checkered cloths were grouped together beneath Chinese lanterns strung between the trees. Music was provided by two violins and a piano on the porch of the building. They no sooner had been seated than a bowing, smiling waiter thrust a menu before them. After they had ordered dinner, Lieutenant Cary rose.

"While we are waiting for our first course I'll call your friends. Be back in a moment."

Lieutenant Cary disappeared into the house and Beverly took note of her surroundings. This was a side of Cuba she would probably never see again. A glance was enough to tell it was not a spot commonly frequented by tourists. How she wished Shirley and Lenora could see it, too.

Lieutenant Cary slid into the seat opposite her and smiled.

"I wish I had more assignments like this. Dinner with a pretty girl——"

A crash and rending of metal came from somewhere

out in front of the house. Lieutenant Cary pushed back his chair and hurried away. Beverly followed him. Out in the glare of automobile lights they saw the wreckage. Their motorcycle had been hurled against a pillar and lay a twisted mass of iron. The cause of the accident was a big, black sedan whose Cuban driver was hysterically explaining that his brakes had failed to work properly.

"There goes our means of travel," the lieutenant muttered to Beverly. "I don't know how I'll get you back to the yacht."

Someone moved through the crowd to Lieutenant Cary's side.

"Permit me to drive you wherever you wish to go," a suave voice suggested. "I am going into town. I shall be happy to have company."

"Thank you, no," Lieutenant Cary replied. "We shall go back to our dinner."

He hurried Beverly to their table.

"I don't understand," Beverly said. "We had a chance for a ride into town. But you——"

"Don't you see how convenient it was?" he asked. "Smash our motorcycle and then take us in their car. Did you notice the license number of the car that smashed our motorcycle? It belonged to your old friend the Countess."

"Then we didn't lose them after all!" Beverly exclaimed. "What do we do now?"

The waiter set their first course before them and the lieutenant grinned.

"We had better eat our dinner while we make plans. Perhaps I can borrow a car."

They gulped most of their dinner, much too anxious to be on their way to wait for any dessert. Lieutenant Cary borrowed a car; though it was ancient and full of squeaks and rattles, it ran, and once more they were on their way. Over dark roads, through brightly lighted city streets and narrow, shadowy ones, they went as swiftly as they dared to the dock. There was a wide expanse of dark water between them and the *Susabella.*

"They're sailing without us!" Beverly said unbelievingly.

"She's adrift," the lieutenant exclaimed in a worried tone. "She'll ram someone. Hey, aboard the *Susabella!*"

Though they shouted no one appeared on deck to heed their warning as the white yacht rode easily on the swell, drifting farther and farther away from shore.

"What will we do?" Beverly asked, just as the headlights of another car burst upon them.

The lieutenant clasped her by the hand and started back toward his borrowed car.

"We're getting out of here."

"Where will we go?" Beverly asked.

They climbed back into the car, turned it around, and started away from the dock. They were proceeding at a fair rate of speed when they came to a cross street and another car bore down upon them. Lieutenant Cary tried vainly to swing his car to the side but a crash was inevitable. There was a shattering of glass, a rending of metal, and the old car toppled over.

Beverly felt a weight against her as the lieutenant tried to protect her from the flying glass. Then everything was a blur of jolts and blackness and half-uttered cries. She was flung out into the street, bruised and scratched. She sat up dazedly as a dark figure crawled from the other sedan and ran limping down the street.

"Miss Gray!" It was Lieutenant Cary's voice. Beverly managed to rise and walk toward the car.

Her companion was half-pinned in the wreckage and Beverly looked about for help.

"Come closer."

She knelt by the lieutenant who managed a faint smile.

"Sorry to get you into this mess."

"I'll get help and have you out in a jiffy," Beverly assured him.

"There isn't time to wait for that. Here, take this." He thrust a thick brown envelope at her. "The good fates must have conspired to have you with me. You've got to get this to the address on the envelope."

"But you——" Beverly began.

"I'll be all right. That car deliberately crashed into ours. The driver will be back in a few moments with his friends. You've got to get away now. His car is still upright. It may run. Try it."

"But I wouldn't know——" Beverly started once more in protest.

"You are all that stands between the Americas and war," he said desperately. "You have to get those papers to Washington. I'm drafting you into service," he added with a weak smile. "Here is some money." He thrust some crumpled bills into her hand. "Go to the airport. Hire a plane and hurry!"

Beverly went across to the car which had hit them. The front bumper was off, one headlight was smashed, the radiator grill was bent and both fenders were rumpled. She slid into the driver's seat and after two attempts the motor coughed into life.

People were beginning to run to the scene, and she knew in a moment there would be a crowd. Much as she hated to leave Lieutenant Cary, hurt as he obviously was, it was his wish that she go on. And if it were true that his enemies had caused the collision, she would not have much time to get away. There would be willing hands to help him, but she was on her own from now on.

By several twists and turns she left the scene of the accident behind her and tried to concentrate on the streets. She had a hazy idea of the way her taxi had gone when she followed Lieutenant Cary earlier in the day, but now, in the darkness, it was hard to distinguish landmarks. However, she went out of her way only once before she found the road leading from the city to the airport.

It was precarious driving with only one headlight to light the unfamiliar roads and in a car which might at any moment break down. It did not occur to Beverly until later that it was also a stolen car.

A maze of thoughts swept through her mind as she drove: what would Larry and the others think—she dare not stop to tell them all that had happened—Lieutenant

Cary pinned under the wreckage of their car—the Countess as she had been watching from her parked car earlier in the evening—the story all this would make for Charlie Blaine and his beloved *Tribune*. Determinedly she tried to put all worry from her and think only of the papers she carried. "All that stands between the Americas and war!" Lieutenant Cary's words echoed in her ears. It couldn't be that urgent, but it was thrilling to think she might have a hand in her country's destiny.

If the drive to the airport had seemed long this afternoon it seemed even longer now. She kept glancing in the rear vision mirror to see if she were being followed, but no one car stayed with her very long and so she felt quite safe. She went several miles past the road leading from the highway to the airport and it took precious time to come back. She left the car at the entrance to the farthest hangar and walked through the darkness to the one building where there was a light. The moon was brilliant overhead. Beverly could see an airplane standing idle at the start of the runway. She thought it must be the one waiting for Lieutenant Cary and went on feeling more confident.

Some instinct must have warned her, however, for before entering the small office building where the light burned, she paused on her way past the window to look inside. She was to be ever grateful that she had done so.

Seated at a small table, reading a newspaper, was a man whom Beverly surmised to be the pilot, since he wore the customary leather jacket and a helmet and goggles lay on the table beside him. At the other side of the table sat the man who had followed the lieutenant from the dock that afternoon. He was writing in a small notebook. Evidently they expected Lieutenant Cary to return and were awaiting him.

A bell rang so suddenly and so close that Beverly jumped. Then she realized the window of the building was open and it was the telephone. The pilot picked up the instrument.

"Hello? Yes? Karl? Just a minute." He handed the telephone to the other man and went back to his newspaper.

Beverly watched, fascinated, while Karl took the telephone.

"Yes?" There was a long, listening pause. Then: "Where? The papers are gone?" At this point Beverly clutched her precious package more tightly. "A girl?"

Karl spoke again. "She will be easier to deal with. We will wait."

The man replaced the receiver and looked at the pilot. "It will not be as difficult as I feared. The girl will undoubtedly come here and want to hire a plane. The rest will be simple." With that he went back to writing in his notebook and silence fell again upon the room.

CHAPTER XVIII

The Brown Envelope

THE airplane stood bathed in cool, bright moonlight, the only object in the long flat expanse of landing field. Beverly approached it slowly, keeping to the shadows of the buildings. Since it was impossible for her to hire the plane and have the pilot take her to the States, a plan was forming in her mind. It was daring and unwise; but, she told herself, the situation called for daring. It might well be her only chance to get away safely.

Could she fly the plane herself? Only a few weeks ago both she and Lenora had depended upon her ability to pilot a plane in order to escape from smugglers. Now, when so much more depended upon her, surely she could fly this small two-seater.

She ran from the shadows of the hangar to the dark protection of the plane's wing and stood there while she debated whether to take the chance. All indecision left her when the door of the office opened and a man came out. He walked to the nearest hangar and soon she heard the squeak of the big doors as they opened. He was probably getting ready to put the plane away for the night.

Beverly pulled the blocks away from the wheels and climbed into the cockpit. The motor broke into a roar and the plane obeyed her slightest touch. As it taxied down the runway she looked back. Two figures were running in its wake, waving and shouting. With an excited laugh Beverly returned their wave and moved the stick back. The little plane climbed eagerly, as if it, too, were anxious to get away. She set a course by the compass on the lighted dial and consulted her fuel supply. The tank was full. She breathed a sigh of relief. If everything went well she should be home tomorrow. Home! New York—White Corners—why, she would be on hand to welcome the *Susabella* when it docked.

All around, above and below, was a sea of moonlight.

It was almost as bright as day, except that there was an ethereal quality about the milk-whiteness that made her look for elves and fairies dancing on her wing tips. On such a night as this she had stood before the Taj Mahal in India. Here, flying high above the world, there was the same quality of being set apart, alone in a strange, unreal world of magical beauty. She had met Larry there, at the Taj Mahal, but she certainly would not meet him tonight.

The plane dipped sharply and Beverly sat up with a jerk. She had fallen asleep for an instant. Now that she was relaxed she realized for the first time how exhausted she was. She looked over the side of the cockpit and saw the sea sparkling far below her. She was over open water. If she dozed off again, there would be slight chance of landing the plane if anything went wrong. Sitting still she became aware of the bruises and scratches she had sustained in the automobile crash, and she was developing a thirst. She thought happily that in the morning she would be able to land somewhere in the States, refuel her plane, and have a good breakfast.

Her second thought was not as pleasant. She would not be able to land. She was flying a stolen plane. Of course it had been "borrowed" in a good cause, but the Countess would be wise enough to have the license number telegraphed to all points the plane would be likely to pass and Beverly would be picked up by the police. That would entail hours of delay and Lieutenant Cary had urged her to hurry. There was nothing to be done but go straight to Washington and fulfill her promise to the lieutenant.

Meanwhile, long empty hours lay ahead of her and she was growing increasingly weary. Her eyes refused to stay open. She had heard of tragic accidents caused by people falling asleep at the wheel of an automobile, but she had never heard of a pilot who had fallen asleep. She tried to sing but the wind whipped her breath away. She tried to plot the story she would write for Charlie Blaine but the thoughts wouldn't come. There was a dull ache in the back of her head and all she wanted to do was sleep—sleep—sleep——

The little plane banked slowly and began to turn, faster and faster. Frantically, Beverly tried to pull the nose of the ship up. The plane trembled with the effort but continued its plunge. Beverly looked over the side. The dark ocean and a strip of sandy beach was dizzily rushing up to meet her. She had no parachute and there probably would have been no time to use it if she did have one. All she could do was try to pull the ship into a glide. She cut off the ignition and tried with all her strength to get the plane out of the spin.

Almost to the ground, it straightened out. There was a snap and the control stick wobbled helplessly in her hand. She had come out of the spin, but there still was no hope of avoiding a crash. She tried desperately to keep the plane on as even a keel as possible while it settled earthward. If only she could overshoot the water and make the beach! All the instructions Larry had given her about making a forced landing were jumbled in her head, but none of them covered landing in the ocean. Frantically Beverly tried to recall what he had said.

A crazy line of song flashed through her mind: "Down went McGinty to the bottom of the sea!" In this case it would be Beverly. "Down went Beverly to the bottom of the sea—right into Davy Jones's lap!"

The little plane acted like a crazy thing, rising and falling, rising and falling again, with the air currents. Luckily there was a tail wind. It might help to carry her to land. It was impossible to pick her own landing place. The plane was completely out of control. All she could do was brace herself for the impact that would come when the plane hit the ground.

The shore was a definite outline now in the first rosy streaks of dawn. Beverly realized she must have flown for hours before she dozed for those fateful seconds that left the plane uncontrolled.

The plane swooped lower and lower, now skimming the waves and again nosing into the air. At last it appeared to settle to a straight course and headed directly for the shore. The ocean licked hungrily at the wheels as the plane hurtled along. The shore was coming closer and closer. At last the plane touched the sand, skimmed along a few feet and stopped abruptly. The tail came up until the plane stood on its nose like a great animal doing fantastic tricks, then crashed over and lay still.

It seemed an eternity before Beverly could pick herself up from the sandbank into which she had been flung. It was a long time, for the sun was high and sea gulls circled noisily overhead when she got dizzily to her feet and stared at the wrecked plane. Her throat was parched and she felt hungry. To move was an effort and the protest of bruised and strained muscles was almost too much to bear.

As far as she could see there was no house, no living thing, except the sea gulls. Sand stretched empty and monotonous on three sides and on the other was the restless, seething sea.

"Now what?" she asked herself.

The hopelessness of her new predicament almost made her give up in despair. But she bolstered her courage and started doggedly to walk to civilization. Sooner or later she must meet someone or come to a town.

The effort to go on grew harder at each step. The sand seemed to cling to her feet and make them heavy to move. Sometimes the ground rose and fell crazily before her, and she had to stand with closed eyes until the giddiness had passed. Once or twice she stumbled headlong into clumps of coarse grass that scratched her face and arms. She went on wearily, and still there was no sign of life. She was alone with the sand, the blazing sun, and the restless sea.

Then, suddenly, there was something else. At first Beverly thought it was a mirage but after a time, when it did not go away, she knew it really was a road—an unpaved, narrow, dusty automobile track, to be sure, but it had to lead somewhere. It was like a new lease on life to see even this faint sign of life and she went on with renewed hope.

She followed the road until it seemed she couldn't go another step. There was more vegetation now and sometimes she stopped to rest in small patches of shade, but still there was no place she could obtain a drink to ease the terrible thirst burning within her.

At last she rounded a corner of the road which was shielded at this point by a high, sandy cliff, and came upon a green and white cottage. It probably was a winter home and at first Beverly was afraid the owner had not yet opened the house for the coming season. Then she saw that the windows were flung wide to the sun and the curtains stirred in the faint breeze. She started forward at a run, as swiftly as her tired legs could carry her. What if this were another mirage, a trick of her tired brain?

When Beverly awoke her first sensation was of delicious warmth and comfort. A cautious peep from half-opened eyes divulged the fact that the sun was streaming in the windows, and on the window sill sat a huge Persian cat industriously washing his already spotless paws. From beyond came the subdued murmur of the sea. It was all very unfamiliar and Beverly sat up for a better look at the room.

"Meow," greeted the cat.

"Meow to you, too," returned Beverly.

She was in a huge four-poster bed facing the double windows. Across the room was a dressing table and bench upholstered in yellow satin. A yellow satin chaise lounge occupied one corner of the room, flanked by crowded bookshelves. The floor was covered by a thick carpet of dark green and the wallpaper was a pale yellow with a green design in it. The room was done simply but in expensive good taste.

Beverly frowned thoughtfully as she tried to recall what had happened since she first viewed the house from down the road. She had run toward it, she knew, until she reached the door. She remembered ringing the bell but after that things were a blur. She must have fainted on the doorstep. She had hazy memories of a tall woman with iron-gray hair and a stern, dry voice, mixed with a gentle but disapproving man called James. She could recall only that they had been very kind to her.

How she had gotten into this room and how long she had been here she did not know. She stepped out of bed and consulted her reflection in the mirror over the dressing table. Her first reaction was to laugh. She had a black eye—a genuine shiner, souvenir, probably, of the automobile accident. Memories of the accident brought back others of Lieutenant Cary and the brown envelope. The brown envelope! Where was it?

Frantically she looked about for her clothes. They were gone. Probably they were no longer presentable, but how far could she get in pink satin pajamas? She pulled the silk cord at the side of the bed. A few seconds later the door opened and a tall distinguished-looking woman entered and came straight to Beverly.

"Feeling better, I see. What would you like for lunch? It is too late for breakfast." Before Beverly could say a word, she continued: "Orange juice, bacon and scrambled eggs and toast all right?"

"Fine," Beverly admitted, wondering how to approach this crisp individual.

"I've sent James to the village for some clothes for you," the dry voice continued. "The ones you wore aren't fit to be seen."

"You're very kind," Beverly said. "When I came here, did I have a brown envelope with me?"

"Yes, you did, and when you were so ill I thought it best to send for the major."

"The major?" Beverly murmured meekly.

"I thought since his name was on the envelope he must be your father or fiancé. I notice you are wearing a diamond ring. Anyway, he will be here at three o'clock."

"He's coming here?"

What would happen next, Beverly wondered. She had been supposed to deliver the envelope to Major King. Now this woman had sent for the major to come here—and he was actually coming!

"The envelope——" Beverly murmured.

"Here." The older woman opened a drawer of the dressing table and lifted out the brown envelope. "I put it there for safekeeping. James is the sort of individual who can't resist peeping into other people's affairs." She looked at Beverly more closely. "That eye looks bad. Does it hurt?"

"No," Beverly admitted.

"I like that," her hostess said firmly. "You aren't squeamish. Well, don't stand there and catch cold. Get back into bed and I'll bring your lunch. Then you must tell me how you came to this forsaken spot." With that she strode out of the room and Beverly was left alone with the cat who solemnly blinked at her while she examined the envelope.

It was still sealed and apparently had not been tampered with. Beverly breathed a sigh of relief and put it under her pillow.

Her hostess came back with a tray of food and while the girl ate she stood by the window and stroked the cat.

"Now," the woman said when Beverly finished the last piece of toast. "Tell me where you are from and how you came to faint on my doorstep."

"I'm sorry about that," Beverly said, blushing, "but, you see——"

"You were exhausted and feverish," her hostess put in firmly. "You looked as though you had been shipwrecked."

"I was," Beverly smiled. To the woman's amazement she went on to tell about the airplane trip from Cuba, eliminating the importance of the brown envelope, thinking it wiser not to divulge it.

"Sounds fantastic," was her hostess' verdict, "but I believe you."

"You haven't told me your name," Beverly said with a smile. "I'd like to know who my good fairy is."

"Beatrice Colfax," was the retort. "This is my winter residence. I arrived here only three days ago so it is fortunate for you that you didn't come last week."

Beatrice Colfax! Beverly reached back into her memory and brought up facts she had learned from time to time during her newspaper career. Beatrice Colfax—a mansion on Fifth Avenue, a fortune in rare paintings, a reputation for an acid tongue and fantastically large gifts to charity, constantly besieged by fortune hunters and supersalesmen. During her fifty years or more she had remained single, traveled around the world, making many acquaintances but scarcely any real friends. She remained aloof and puzzling to the press. Many had sought to publish her true life story but none had been able to glean other than the bare facts.

Now Beverly felt suddenly awe-stricken and timid in this woman's presence.

"Well?" Miss Colfax demanded crisply. "Cat got your tongue?"

Beverly smiled uncertainly. "I work for a newspaper, you know. I was mentally reviewing our file on you."

To her surprise Miss Colfax laughed.

"To my credit, I hope." She went closer to the window. "Here comes James." She disappeared into the hall and in a moment returned with James, a meek little man and very much the correct butler, who put his packages down on the chaise lounge and left the room. Miss Colfax opened them and helped Beverly to dress.

When Beverly viewed herself in the mirror she was very pleased. A brown tweed suit, alligator pumps, and a golden yellow blouse—all of which were vastly becoming.

"How can I thank you?" Beverly murmured. "You've gone to so much trouble."

"Nonsense! Don't thank me, I hate gratitude. It has been an adventure for me, too. Come along downstairs. It is almost time for your major to arrive."

Beverly took her precious brown envelope and followed her hostess downstairs into a cool and airy sitting room whose windows overlooked the sea. Beverly was wondering how she would talk to this brisk person when James announced:

"Major King, Madame."

A tall, forceful-looking man in army uniform strode

in. He bowed stiffly to Miss Colfax and then to Beverly.

"Now, Miss Colfax, may I ask what this is about?" he demanded. "I was on my way to Cuba when I received your message and since it didn't take me far out of my way, I decided to come and see what it was you wanted."

"But," Miss Colfax began in amazement. "This girl—don't you recognize her?"

Major King turned his puzzled glance on Beverly.

"I have never seen her before."

"You haven't?" Miss Colfax echoed. "Young woman, explain yourself."

"I think, Major," Beverly said, "this will explain for me." She handed him the brown envelope and waited.

After he had opened the envelope and read snatches of the report it contained, he sat down beside Beverly.

"Where did you get this, young woman?"

"From a man who called himself Lieutenant Cary," Beverly explained.

"But where is he? Why hasn't be notified us? Why did he give this to you?"

While the sea murmured outside and Miss Colfax listened wide-eyed, Beverly told the major her story.

"Highly irregular, highly irregular," the major murmured when she had finished. "We have an unconfirmed report that Lieutenant Cary is in the hospital. That is why I was going to Cuba. You've done a good job, Miss Gray."

"It was my intention to bring the papers to you in Washington," Beverly told him. "Your coming here is like the mountain going to Mohammed."

"Well, Miss Mohammed," the major laughed, "if you ever need the services of the Army Intelligence Department, you need only call on me."

"I need them now," Beverly said. "How am I going to get back to New York?"

"You may drive back with me," the major offered, rising. "We shall be on our way at once."

Miss Colfax walked to the door with them, briskly refusing Beverly's grateful thanks.

"Just don't write anything about me for that newspaper of yours," she commanded.

"The best stories never get written," Beverly complained. "I'd like to write about you and this lovely house by the sea."

"And make the people who think I'm queer change all their ideas? I forbid you!"

"What's the good of having adventures if you can't tell about them?" Beverly wanted to know. "Major King won't let me write about the mission Lieutenant Cary was on, either. How am I to explain where I've been?"

"Tell anyone who asks that it is none of their business," Miss Colfax returned, "and come and see me in New York, you amazing girl."

Major King led the way to his car. There were three other army men there, young officers who snapped into polite attention when the major presented them to Beverly. She sat in the back seat with two of them and the major got in front with the driver.

Beverly smiled to herself when she thought how her adventure had started—alone, hunted and mysterious, and now she was homeward bound with an army escort. This would be something to tell Lenora!

CHAPTER XIX

Home Again

LOIS flung her magazine aside and paced restlessly to the window. A rainy Saturday was awful, she told herself gloomily. She didn't feel like sketching or shopping. Her books failed to hold her interest and there wasn't even Lenora to argue with.

Connie Elwood opened the door and stuck her head in. "Hi!"

"Come in and chase the blue goblins away," Lois implored. "I am about to die of boredom."

"I," Connie announced, "have to buy a fall hat. Come along and help."

"I'm not in the mood," Lois shook her head.

"Any more news from Lenora?"

"Nothing since the cable," Lois replied. She picked up the much folded cablegram and read it again although she already had memorized it.

"'Home Sunday you lucky people.'"

Connie smiled. "I couldn't spend as much time on a boat as they do. I hate the water. I prefer to keep my feet on good old Mother Earth."

"What about the bathtub?" Lois giggled and dodged the newspaper Connie flung at her. She wandered to the window. "If only it would stop raining! Hello, what's this?"

"What?" Instantly Connie was beside her friend.

"A car—and soldiers!" Lois murmured.

"And—why, it's Beverly!" Connie gasped.

There was a concerted rush for the door and both girls dashed madly down the stairs. They met Beverly at the front door and both hugged her at once.

Then Connie asked: "Hey, where's your convoy?"

"My what?" Beverly laughed.

"Your escort—the army!" Connie continued. "I like a man in a uniform."

"What were you doing that the army had to bring you home?" Lois asked suspiciously. "What were you up to?"

"It is a long story," Beverly said, "and if you want to hear it you have to feed me."

Over a piece of Lois' chocolate cake and a glass of milk Beverly recounted the events from the moment the *Susabella* docked at Havana to her arrival at Mrs. Callahan's.

"They brought you all the way home?"

"Probably so they could keep an eye on you," Lois grinned. "To see that you really were what you said you were."

"I never thought of that," Beverly exclaimed.

"What do you propose to do now?" Connie murmured.

"I'm going down to see Charlie Blaine," Beverly said. "Then I'm going to walk up and down Broadway until I am convinced that I'm really home again. After that I think I'll go out to White Corners."

"Would you rather go alone, or may we tag along with you?" Connie asked.

"You know Shirley expressed her car from California," added Lois. "We've been using it since she's been away, and we could drive you to White Corners."

"I'd like that," Beverly said. She looked around the familiar kitchen and sighed. "My, it is good to be back. I want to have lunch at Smitty's, walk in Central Park, ride the subway, and dodge traffic in Times Square and——"

"That is quite enough for a starter," Connie laughed. "What are we waiting for?"

"Funny," Lois said as they donned raincoats and rubbers, "I don't feel a bit gloomy now. All I needed was to see one of my chums."

"Tell me what the other girls are doing," Beverly proposed.

As they walked along arm in arm, the one in the middle holding the umbrella, Lois and Connie brought Beverly up to date on the doings of the other Alpha Delta girls.

"And, Bev," Lois finished mischievously, "I think Connie is about to become engaged."

"I am not!" Connie denied. "Well, not right now, anyway."

"Is it that nice Grant Phillips?" Beverly asked.

Connie nodded, her cheeks pink. "But he is still in medical school and after that comes his interneship. It will be years before anything definite——"

"That's why I say it must be love," Lois declared. "If you intend to wait all that time——"

"How about yourself?" Connie retorted. "You and Paul are——"

"Time!" Beverly called laughingly. "I don't see how you girls get along without a referee."

"Oh, we don't really mean all we say," Lois told her brightly.

They had reached the *Tribune* building at this point and Connie and Lois followed Beverly inside. Beverly's arrival called for an abrupt termination of duties while her fellow workers crowded around her. Everyone from the copy boy to the editor himself had a welcome greeting for her. Then, at last, the girls were alone with Charlie Blaine in his office.

"The wanderer returneth!" he beamed on her. "Your stories were swell, Beverly. I guess I'll have to make you a roving reporter."

"I'd love it," Beverly returned.

"I had a cable from Lenora," he continued. "She says she has enough pictures to keep our paper supplied for months."

"The *Susabella* docks tomorrow," Lois smiled.

"And we'll really give them a reception," Blaine laughed. "I'm sending photographers down to meet Lenora."

"All the Alpha girls are going," added Connie. "Now if we only had a band——"

"I'll get one," Blaine promised. "My kid brother has one—fancy uniforms and all."

"And we'll have confetti and flowers," Lois plotted. "Oh, boy!"

The plot grew after the girls had left the *Tribune* office and had luncheon. Afterward they walked uptown through the pouring rain. The streets shone in the wetness and umbrellas crowded together like mushrooms. The gutters were running rivers and rain obscured the shop windows.

"If you really were a roving reporter, Bev, I'll bet you would get to cover everything exciting," Lois murmured.

"Right now I'm going with Connie to buy a hat," Beverly laughed.

"That will be exciting enough, what with the new styles," Connie added.

They spent the rest of the afternoon shopping, in and

out of stores, trying on hats. Connie didn't find any that pleased her, but Beverly and Lois each selected one.

Later, when the rain had stopped and the air and sky promised a clear day tomorrow, the girls stopped at Smitty's for dinner; and then, with Lois at the wheel of Shirley's car, they drove out to White Corners, prowling about for hours. They peeped into the rooms, where hours before workmen had been busy with alterations and painting, and eagerly helped Beverly with advice on color schemes.

When they returned to Mrs. Callahan's, Kathleen, Hope, and Virginia were there, with a pan of newly made fudge and a pitcher of lemonade, playing Chinese checkers. The game was abruptly deserted and the lights burned far into the night while the girls talked.

The next morning they went to the dock early and spent restless hours pacing up and down until the *Susabella* came into sight. Lenora nearly went headfirst over the side of the boat waving at them.

"Yoo hoo! Here we are!"

"Look at the people on the pier!" Shirley gasped. "There's Beverly!"

"And Lois and Connie and—and a band!" Lenora cried

as the musicians Charlie Blaine had secured for the occasion broke into a melody. "Oh, my goodness!"

Lines were made taut and the gangplank pushed into place. Lenora and Shirley were the first to rush off the boat, straight into the arms of their friends. As Lenora had desired, there were huge bouquets of flowers from the girls, and Blaine's photographers did a good job of teasing Lenora by snapping her from the most ridiculous angles.

"Maybe we didn't have a time while you were racing around Havana!" Lenora pounced upon Beverly. "Somebody set the *Susabella* adrift while we were dancing at the hotel and we practically had to call out the navy to get a motorboat to go after it. Then Lieutenant Cary sent word to us from the hospital that you were flying home and—my goodness, what excitement!"

It was the happiest kind of reunion. Everyone was safe and each was anxious to tell what had happened since the last time they were together. The musicians and photographers departed and still the group continued to stand in the middle of the dock and chatter until Lenora made an announcement:

"I'm hungry."

"Me, too," Jim said.

"We've arranged with Smitty for lunch," Connie told the new arrivals. "Let's go."

"Wait a minute! Where's Beverly and Larry?" Lois asked.

There was a hurried glance around. Beverly and Larry were seated on a packing case a little apart, talking.

"Do you want to be alone or could we interest you in a little food?" Lenora called.

Larry jumped to his feet and held out his hands to Beverly.

"We were wondering when someone would say something important," he returned laughingly.

In addition to the two cars in which the Alpha Delta girls had come to the pier, the young people had to press taxis into service to take the whole group uptown. At Smitty's they took over the restaurant while the proprietress beamed in approval.

"It's good to be home," Shirley declared.

"You wouldn't believe how dull it was while you were away," Lois declared, looking at the smiling faces about the table.

"Then you missed us!" Lenora said triumphantly.

"How could we help it?" Connie laughed. "We aren't used to such peace and quiet."

"From now on you won't have much of it," Lenora promised. "We are here to stay for a while."

At this point we will take leave of Beverly and her friends to meet them again involved in more mysterious adventures in Beverly Gray's Problem.

THE BEVERLY GRAY
MYSTERY STORIES